THE MOTHERS' BOARD: MOTHERS KNOW BEST

LaShaunda K. Jackson-Williams

ISBN: 1541004884
ISBN 13: 9781541004887

All Scripture quotations are taken from the King James Version of the Bible. (Public Domain.)

This book is a work of fiction. Any references to historical events, real people, or real places are used fictitiously. Other names, characters, names, places, and events are products of the author's imagination, and any resemblance to actual events or places or persons living or dead is entirely coincidental.

ACKNOWLEDGEMENTS

I would like to acknowledge with gratitude the memory of my beautiful grandmothers, Mrs. Thelma Martin and Mrs. Ruby Lee Jones; and my lovely great-aunt, Sylvia Madden. Thank you for sharing your love, lives, and work on the Mothers' Board at God's Lighthouse Community Church.

I am grateful to my amazing parents, Rev. Robert and Mrs. Evelyn Jackson. You kept me grounded and this book would not have been possible without you. Thank you!

To my husband, Dr. Derek Williams, thank you for your countless support and love throughout this journey.

Special thanks to Barbara Leonard.

Finally, this book is dedicated to all the church mothers and mothers' boards in the world. Your passion for Christ and the Church is my inspiration for this book. I pray that you are remembered and regarded with the warmest appreciation whenever this book is read.

SUNDAY-MORNING MAYHEM

With ten minutes before the start of morning worship, members and friends of One Way Church of the Lord hurried through the torrential rain and pounding thunder to the main doors of the sanctuary, where they rushed to fill the pews facing the empty pulpit. As the musicians kept the nicely dressed congregation distracted with their soul-stirring and foot-stomping melodies, the deacons sat behind closed doors, looking grim while discussing how to deliver the bad news to the congregation. In the midst of the potential madness, the deacons struggled to get the story straight, with the knowledge that outside the door, a sanctuary full of unsuspecting people would soon be demanding answers.

In the pews some members sat chatting together, holding small children in their laps, while others sat quietly, waiting for the service to start. Ushers buzzed through the sanctuary, seating members and passing out fans and programs.

Suddenly the double doors in the rear of the sanctuary flew open, and the music ceased. Silence filled the room as the congregation twisted and turned in their seats to see who was entering. Deacon Evans, chairman of the Deacons' Board, marched into the church, followed by the other six deacons. As they proceeded down the main aisle of the church, a hushed silence followed their footsteps on the plush red carpet that paved the way from the back of the sanctuary

1

to the front of the church. All eyes remained on the deacons as they walked onto the stage and stood side by side facing the congregation. At first this seemed to be a normal Sunday-morning service led by the deacons, but the somber looks on the deacons' faces revealed otherwise.

Deacon Evans approached the podium. He cleared his throat and spoke: "Members, I regret to inform you that Pastor Walker has resigned as pastor of One Way effective immediately."

In the congregation some cried, some prayed, some shouted in disgust, and some got up and left the church. One thing was certain: the majority of the congregation did not greet this news with happiness.

Deacon Evans nearly shouted to be heard over the tumult: "Church, don't rush to judgment until you have heard all of the facts. Give us a chance to report the facts. Please settle down!"

At the cacophony of frustrated sighs, moans, and cries from the congregation, Deacon Evans waved his hand to make it stop—but it didn't.

Deacon Carter, who towered over all the other deacons, nudged Deacon Evans aside and shouted in a deep baritone voice, "Order in the church!"

The congregation snapped their eyes forward and hushed to a complete quiet. Deacon Carter smiled, showing his perfect pearly teeth. He nodded at Deacon Evans as he stepped away from the podium.

"Thank you, brother," Deacon Evans said. "Members, as of last Sunday night, One Way has not had any contact with Pastor Walker. He has been unreachable despite numerous attempts to get in touch with him. On Wednesday Pastor Walker was a no-show for prayer meeting and Bible study. Yesterday morning Pastor Walker was a no-show for the missionary meeting and the annual Mothers' Board Brunch. This morning Pastor Walker did not call in or show up for Sunday school or morning worship service. We the deacons of One Way Church of the Lord have concluded that Pastor Walker has abandoned his position. Deacon Miller will now provide the results of his investigation to you."

Stepping aside, Deacon Evans made way for Deacon Miller, the short, single, gossiping, snooping, soft-spoken deacon with selective hearing. Deacon Miller made his way to the podium and adjusted the microphone with one hand while pulling a little black leather-bound notebook from his coat pocket with his other hand. After clearing his throat and flipping through his notes that he had compiled with care that morning, Deacon Miller addressed the congregation:

"Good morning, members. On a weekly basis I drive by Pastor Walker's house to make sure things are in order. Around 2:00 p.m. yesterday when I pulled up to Pastor Walker's home, I saw a *For Rent* sign in the front window. I then walked up to Pastor Walker's porch and saw that all of his curtains were missing. As I glanced into the window from the porch, I saw no furniture. Members, every room, closet, and cupboard in that house was empty. I knocked on the front and the back doors, and no one answered. I spoke with Pastor Walker's neighbors—Mr. and Mrs. White. They told me that Pastor Walker moved out in the middle of the night sometime last week. They also said they did not wish to get involved with the matters of One Way and Pastor Walker. They then asked me to get off their grass. When I tried to get more information, they rushed inside their tan 2001 Dodge Caravan and sped off."

Deacon Miller paused, cleared his throat again, and went on. "I then approached the home of Pastor Walker's other neighbor, Ms. Roxie, the nosy old woman who spotted me the minute I pulled up to Pastor's house. I asked her if she knew what happened to Pastor Walker, and I was told verbatim, 'Why you asking me a question you already know the answer to? You folks at that church get your kicks out of getting rid of pastors. I know your game.' Then she shouted at the top of her lungs, 'You're nothing but the devil in sheep's clothing. I rebuke you, Satan! Satan, get off my property!' She raised both of her hands up to the sky and shouted, 'Satan, I rebuke you! Get off my property! Get off my property before I call the police!' After a crowd from the neighborhood had gathered around, I ran to my car and headed home to make telephone calls.

"I first called the phone number on the *For Rent* sign, which ended up being a local realtor who refused to give me any personal information on Pastor Walker. I also called Pastor's home phone number and cell phone number, but both had been disconnected. I then called Pastor's mother, Aretha Walker. She cussed me out and then hung up on me. I called her back and she cussed me out again before hanging up. I then called one of Pastor's brother, Dale Walker, in Memphis. He cussed at me for two minutes and twelve seconds straight before he hung up on me. Members, this concludes my report."

With some people shaking their heads in disbelief, the congregation sat there, remaining quiet as they waited for more information.

Deacon Evans returned to the podium and thanked Deacon Miller for his extensive report. Meanwhile a flow of constant chatter erupted from the second pew. The first pew belonged to the Deacons' Board. The second pew was something special, as it belonged to the esteemed Mothers' Board. Directly above the mothers' pew hung three remote-controlled ceiling fans, and the pew itself had been outfitted with a two-inch Serta memory foam cushion expressly for the mothers' comfort.

"What extensive report?" Mother Millie said. "The man was just being plain nosey trying to dig up dirt on Pastor Walker. What man drives by another man's home weekly without stopping in to say hello? Somebody up to no good."

"Mothers, hush up so we can hear!" Mother Janie whispered.

Ignoring the chatter, Deacon Miller nodded at Deacon Evans as he placed his little black book in his coat pocket and then returned to the line of deacons behind the podium.

"Excellent work, Deacon Miller," Deacon Evans said, then told the congregation, "Members and friends, it is sufficient to say that Pastor Walker has abandoned his position. We the deacons would like to move forward without haste and appoint an interim pastor until we can hire a permanent pastor."

The members of One Way began murmuring and shouting, showing their outrage at this disappointing news. Miss Lillian, the long standing, never-been-married church secretary, yelled in a high-pitched voice that came out as squeaky and strained: "Excuse me! Excuse me! Excuse me, Deacons! That is incorrect. As Pastor Walker's secretary I would not have spent virtually the entire evening last Sunday confirming the church's fall and winter calendar. Pastor Walker and I spent most of that evening discussing next year's church events. So I don't agree with your assessment of this matter."

The congregation fell silent at the words of Miss Lillian—a soft-spoken, short, skinny woman with chin-length auburn hair, fake eyelashes, and drawn-in eyebrows the shape of a rainbow.

Clenching his jaw at her comments, Deacon Evans walked down off the stage to approach Miss Lillian with a stern stare, and then motioned to her with his index finger, pointing to the rear of the church while snapping the fingers of his other hand. Miss Lillian dropped her Bible on the pew, grabbed her notepad and pen, and got up from her seat.

As Miss Lillian and Deacon Evans walked to the rear of the church, Lulabelle, Deacon Evans' wife and chairwoman of the church's Trustee Board, smiled and winked in approval of her husband's swift removal of the loud woman from the sanctuary.

At the same time, Deacon King approached the microphone and asked the members to allow Deacon Evans and Miss Lillian a moment to confer in private. The members, all still quiet except for a few whispers, watched as Miss Lillian and Deacon Evans departed the sanctuary.

In the church vestibule Deacon Evans placed his index finger in Miss Lillian's face and told her, "You need to keep your big mouth shut! I am running this and don't need your help. This is exactly why your crazy behind can't get a man, because you don't know when to shut up!"

"First of all," Miss Lillian said, her confidence rising, "you don't scare me, Deacon Evans. And as long as God allows me to stand on behalf of my beloved One Way, I will keep telling the truth whether you like it or not."

Deacon Evans frowned, grabbed her arm with alarming force, and told her she better watch herself.

Miss Lillian jerked away and glared at Deacon Evans. "If you value the air you breathe, you will never put your hands on me again!"

Seemingly amused by Miss Lillian's response, Deacon Evans just laughed and called her "foolish" as he followed her back into the sanctuary. As Miss Lillian took her seat, she pressed her lips together, feeling the steaming anger deep within rise to her face. As tears soon rolled down her cheeks and onto the pages of her Bible, Miss Lillian began to read aloud John 6:70—"'Jesus answered them, Have not I chosen you twelve, and one of you is a devil?'" As she continued to recite the verse, the other folks seated on her pew cleared it.

"I wonder what happened. Miss Lillian looks scared straight," Mother Janie whispered to Mother Mae.

Meanwhile, as Deacon Evans returned to the stage, the congregation began to grow agitated again—no doubt because Pastor Walker was the fiftieth pastor at One Way, and the members wanted some stability and longevity from a new pastor. Pastor Walker had only been at One Way for six short months, but the vast majority of members had viewed his appointment as a great fit for both the church and Pastor Walker.

With all the commotion in the congregation, Deacon Evans tried speaking over everyone with a louder voice, but to no avail. Gripping the sides of the podium, he put his lips to the microphone and shouted, "I need for you all to shut up and listen!"

Once again the congregation settled down, but not without a number of astonished looks from those who seemed to feel personally assaulted by his harsh words. Deacon Evans took note of the angry-looking members staring back at him, changed his tone, and offered an apology for his outburst before moving on to make his motion to appoint an interim pastor.

But before he could finish, a female voice called out, "May I speak?"

The woman was Mother Mae, one of One Way Church's eldest members and the chairwoman of the Mothers' Board. Deacon Evans gave an irritated sigh, but he knew the congregation in their current state would hang him if he did not let Mother Mae have her say. He gave a curt nod.

A stout woman in her late seventies, with cotton-colored hair styled in a short bob, Mother Mae grimaced as she rose from her seat. With a firm grip on the back of the pew, she proceeded to speak.

But Mother Janie interrupted: "Give Mother Mae the microphone so she can be heard."

Deacon Evans gave another frustrated sigh, then passed the microphone down to a frowning Mother Janie, who snatched it from him and then turned to gently place it in Mother Mae's hand with a warm smile.

"Thank you, Mother Janie," said Mother Mae as she smiled. She cleared her throat and said, "Deacons, members, and friends, I am truly saddened about what we have all heard this morning, but let's not forget, the deacons alone do not decide who becomes pastor or interim pastor of One Way. They have done this in the past, and our sacred church has become a revolving door."

Back in line with the other deacons, Deacon Evans placed his hand on his hip and raised his nose up in the air at Mother Mae's comments.

But Mother Mae continued, "We as a congregation must decide. I personally think we need to take more time to find out about Pastor Walker's situation before we move to find another pastor. Pastor Walker's situation must be given full consideration. I think we should look into this as a church."

Mother Janie rose to her feet. "Amen, Mother Mae! Let's look into it," she said. She was Mother Mae's best friend and a fellow Mothers' Board member. "Something just isn't right with this story, you hear me?" With one hand on her hip, Mother Janie looked around. "Sound like somebody is lying up in God's house. We got to look into this mess." With her free hand she pointed toward Deacon Evans.

"Did that woman just point over here at us?" Deacon Evans whispered to Deacon King.

"Nah, I believe she was pointing directly at you, Deacon Evans," Deacon King said. And then he scooted away from him.

The other mothers, dressed in their two-piece white suits and white hats, rose to their feet while pointing toward Deacon Evans and shouting such comments as, "Amen and something ain't right!"

Mother Mae thanked the mothers for their support, then faced forward and asked, "May I continue from the stage?"

The deacons nodded, then took their seats as Mother Mae trudged her way up front to the podium.

Mother Mae said, "I'd like to give honor to God, who is the head of my life. Members, I want you all to know that I love One Way. God and this church have been good to my family and me. This is the only church I know. My parents and grandparents attended here, and now my kids, grandchildren, and great-grandchildren attend here. Our church has seen many pastors over the last thirty years. What we have witnessed in the last five to ten years has been awfully embarrassing. One Way has lost credibility in the community and right here in our own church amongst our members. How can we expect sinners to come and accept Christ when our pews are infested with sin?"

"Oh, preach, Mother Mae!" Mother Kellie shouted.

Mother Mae went on. "Back when my father was a deacon, pastors stayed until they retired or died. Now pastors come so quickly and often, the Mothers' Board has to call and remind each other of the current pastor's name. Poor Mother Addie. She is still confused about who our pastor is. I remember when Reverend Jefferson was our pastor back in the '70s. Everything felt right because Reverend Jefferson loved everybody and everybody loved and supported Reverend Jefferson. Reverend Jefferson was a gentle but firm disciplinarian. He did not allow deacons to show up thirty minutes late for service."

The congregation's eyes shifted to Deacon Evans.

"He did not allow choir members to sing if they did not attend choir rehearsal."

Shouts of "Amen" could be heard throughout the sanctuary. However, some of the choir members looked down at their laps.

"Now we have deacons that show up late and leave early, and choir members who lead solos and shout through half of the song because they don't know the words. Reverend Jefferson corrected our children back then, and we were glad about it. Reverend Jefferson would not ask you to do something he was not willing to do. Reverend Jefferson preached and taught love. Once we lost Reverend Jefferson, all hell broke loose."

Mother Millie jumped from her seat and shouted, "Say that again, Mother Mae!"

With a shy grin Mother Mae said, "All hell broke loose." She paused and then continued. "Pastor Walker was selected as One Way's pastor from a pool of over thirty candidates. Remember, ten of the applicants wanted a hefty contract, with a house, car, credit card, and a percentage of each offering, plus a salary. Pastor Walker stood out because of his love for the Lord and his passion for all people. He was not concerned about the money, or how many tithing members were on our membership roll; he was concerned about our souls. He came to the interview in a nicely pressed suit and old, but shining, shoes. He had a down-to-earth calmness that overtook our congregation. Many of the candidates for pastor came to One Way with an entourage or a fancy car, but Pastor Walker arrived with his lively seventy-eight-year-old momma, Mrs. Aretha Walker, in his old, but clean, pickup truck. After he preached that soul-stirring sermon, he led eight souls to Christ. It did not hurt that Pastor Walker had a voice like Barry White either. When he sang 'Amazing Grace,' you felt amazing grace."

Members began nodding in agreement with Mother Mae.

"At that point we the mothers knew that Pastor Walker was our pastor. He was voted in and installed as One Way Church's fiftieth pastor on that first Sunday in November. Pastor Walker stood proud with his momma. Members, does Pastor Walker sound like a man who would abandon his position and church?"

Shouts of "No" echoed throughout the sanctuary.

"I don't think so either, and we must be careful not to judge—because God is the only judge at One Way. You hear me: God is the only judge at One Way. Let's pray that our pastor is found and returned to One Way. God bless you all."

Mother Mae passed the microphone back to Deacon Evans and then she gamboled down the steps to return to her seat. The congregation applauded, and the other mothers welcomed her back to her seat with clapping and shouts of "Amen!"

Just as Deacon Evans was about to speak, Mother Kellie overpowered him with her loud voice: "Father! Father! Father! I am in agreement with Miss Lillian and Mother Mae: Pastor Walker did not abandon his position."

This time Deacon Evans grunted to himself, then shoved a hand inside his pants pocket and nodded for Mother Kellie to continue.

"Last Sunday morning," Mother Kellie said, "prior to morning service Brother Ben and I met with Pastor Walker for our final premarital counseling session. Pastor Walker agreed to officiate our wedding and we set a date for September."

Mother Kellie walked up to the podium as she was speaking, gently pushed Deacon Evans out of the way, and adjusted the microphone to her height.

She continued as Deacon Evans rolled his eyes at her. "Here is what I recall: Brother Ben and I had just completed our final premarital counseling session with Pastor Walker while Sunday school was conducted in the next room. Our premarital counseling sessions normally end thirty minutes prior to the benediction of Sunday school to allow Pastor Walker to make it to Sunday school to offer comments. But because this was our final time with him, this session would end at the approximate time Sunday school ends. This allowed time for us to discuss getting married at the church and setting a date. So I concur with Mother Mae's suggestion to have this matter looked into."

Talking continued amongst the congregation as Mother Kellie walked down off the stage. Brother Ben smiled at Mother Kellie as she took her seat next to him.

Back at the podium, Deacon Evans said, "We the deacons and trustees have looked into Pastor Walker's departure and have now reported our findings to you this morning. So, look, if you would like the matter further investigated, then you may do so on your own time, with your own money. We will not stand in anyone's way of initiating an inquiry regarding Pastor Walker's departure, but we the deacons and trustees are focusing on expeditiously obtaining leadership for our church. I repeat: the deacons and the trustees are moving forward with replacing Pastor Walker. Look, we know what is best for One Way. Let us do our job."

Moans and murmurs rose from the congregation.

Deacon Evan raised his hands and motioned for the congregation to settle down. "Members, before I—excuse me, I mean before *we* move forward with interviewing and hiring a new pastor, we promise to include the membership in the entire process. We are going to do this as a church family with a united front. God knows that I love each and every one of you. We are brothers and sisters in Christ." He paused to let his words sink in with the congregation, pointing toward the congregation and moving his hand from left to right. "God has our back on this! Let's do this together, with God. This is the only way I would want it done."

As Deacon Evans placed one hand over his heart, he spoke softly into the microphone: "As God is my witness, I love this church as much as all of you and I would never do anything to hurt One Way. I promise to make no moves without first consulting my beloved One Way congregation. I have the love of Jesus deep down in my soul. You hear me? Deep! Deep! Deep! Down in my soul! I loved Pastor Walker as much as every one of you. You hear me? I loved Pastor Walker! Church, we must think about this: What would Pastor Walker want us to do? More than that, what does God want us to do? I promise we are going to get through this rough patch together."

Now blank stares came from the pews. The congregation seemed unsure about what had just transpired, and allowed Deacon Evans to continue.

"Members, in light of today's events, we are cancelling morning worship. Let's go home and just be at rest with God on the Sabbath. Please stand for prayer and the benediction."

As Mother Millie got up from her seat, she looked down the pew at the other mothers, made a motion of raising a cup to her mouth, and whispered, "I bet he been hitting that bottle."

Mother Addie shook her head. "Let's give him a chance," she whispered. "Maybe he has changed. You know we've been praying for him for so many years, and maybe we finally got a breakthrough."

Just before Deacon Evans started the prayer, Mother Janie laughed and then whispered, "All hell *is* about to break loose. Mothers, mark my words."

NONSTOP DRAMA

The next morning, as frightening thunderstorms rolled through the town of One Way, Mother Kellie and Brother Ben sat in her kitchen, enjoying their coffee and reading the latest edition of *The One Way Times*. Mother Kellie stumbled upon the following advertisement in the classified section and sat in shocked silence as she read:

PASTOR WANTED IMMEDIATELY!

A local historical African American church in One Way is in desperate need of a pastor. Church has an active membership of 500+. Selected candidate must: be a professional, family-oriented individual; be free of any criminal background activities; exhibit great leadership and teaching abilities; be a team builder and team player; be able to follow directions and report to various high-ranking church officials; be able to conduct meetings and form civic partnerships; have experience counseling individuals and groups; have five years of pastoral or assistant pastoral experience; and provide five references. Special consideration will be

given to African American males with musical talent.
Position will be filled quickly....

The ad went on to list the contact information for "LE/Trustee Chairwoman," to whom candidates could send a resume, salary requirement, and references.

When she finished reading, Mother Kellie looked up from her paper and peered over her the top of her reading glasses at Brother Ben. "Oh my goodness, you won't believe this! Those words he spoke Sunday meant absolutely nothing. The man is a liar—a bald-faced liar," Mother Kellie shouted, shaking her head.

Brother Ben put down the Local section of the paper. "Okay, dear, I won't believe it, so just tell me."

Mother Kellie stood up, took her glasses off, and said, "They went ahead and placed an ad in the paper for a pastor!"

Now Brother Ben's eyes went wide. He pushed his coffee away and said, "You got to be kidding, right? After Deacon Evans touched his heart and confessed his love to One Way and promised to keep us all involved? Are you sure this isn't some other church advertisement?"

"Sorry, Ben, the proof is right here." Mother Kellie folded the newspaper in half so the ad showed and then shoved it in Brother Ben's hands. "No no no! I just can't believe it. I can't believe he'd go and do that!" she said.

Letting her rant, Brother Ben scanned the article, then slammed the paper down on the table. "I have lost all respect for that man! His word means nothing."

"Exactly! And you know what else this means? The *Times* goes to print early on Sunday evenings, right? So they had already submitted this advertisement to the newspaper when he gave us that song and dance yesterday!" She clucked her tongue and said, "Mm-mm-mm!"

Brother Ben shook his head. "Kellie, that man is conniving and dangerous. Clearly he will do and say anything to get his way."

"Amen to that!" Mother Kellie said as she began pacing the kitchen floor.

A moment later she picked up the phone and called the mothers one by one, informing them of the advertisement. This sneaky tactic by Deacon Evans prompted the mothers to launch their own private investigation into Pastor Walker's departure, to be sure the deacons' and trustees' rush to replace Pastor Walker had nothing to do with his disappearance. The mothers knew this task would require a clever plan.

So the mothers met Wednesday evening after weekly Bible study, diving right into a discussion about their private investigation. Plenty angry, but still saddened by Deacon Evans' betrayal, Mother Kellie stood up and led the meeting.

"The timing of Pastor Walker's disappearance and the rush to name a new pastor could hardly be a coincidence," she said.

The mothers all nodded in agreement, a few saying, "That's right" or "Mm-hm."

Mother Mae spoke up then: "That's my presumption as well. So we first must verify that Pastor Walker voluntarily walked away from being pastor at One Way."

After giving a nod, Mother Kellie continued. "Mothers, I suggest we speak to Pastor Walker's family and neighbors. If we use a little finesse, we should be able to get more information—more than Deacon Miller and the others, certainly! I believe their approach was arrogant, and that is why they were unsuccessful in obtaining meaningful information. Mother Mae, Mother Janie, Mother Millie, and I will work on contacting the family and neighbors of Pastor Walker. The rest of you should work on contacting members of the congregation to find out what the rumor mill is reporting about Pastor Walker's departure and whether anyone in the church is involved."

The mothers nodded their assent as they drank coffee.

Then Mother Mae added, "Mothers, it is imperative that we use caution and good judgment about whom we talk to and what questions we ask. Please, as you talk to each person, write down when it is, and whom you talk to and what they say. This will help us keep the facts straight during our investigation. Please remember this matter is confidential. We can't even discuss this with our children or our trusted van driver, Deacon King. Understood?"

The mothers replied "Understood" or "Yes, that's right" or "That's good."

Now Mother Janie stood up and said, "I think we should search Pastor Walker's home. God knows, he could be tied up and stuffed in a closet. I have been watching *Matlock* and *Murder, She Wrote* for more than twenty years. I *know* how to conduct an investigation. You know, there could be clues all over that house."

Many of the other mothers looked at each other with uncomfortable glances, but then Mother Kellie shouted, "Good idea!" She looked to her left and said, "Hey, Mother Addie, are you still good at picking locks?"

"I still know a few tricks," Mother Addie said. Then a brief smirk danced across her face.

"Good!" Mother Kellie said. She paced the floor at the head of the table and mumbled, "Mothers, I promise we will get to the bottom of this mess."

෧

On the following Saturday morning, Mother Mae struggled to get up and get dressed before her oldest son, Eddie, arrived to take her to Food Club. Finally she finished, just as his pickup truck pulled in. As always he waited by the passenger door for her.

"Morning, Eddie," replied Mother Mae, smiling at him. As she climbed in the truck, she commented on how nice and cool it was inside the vehicle.

Eddie closed her door, got in, and said, "Momma, now you know I always want to make sure you are comfortable."

"But, Eddie, I don't want you to get too cold."

Eddie smiled at her. "Momma, I'll be okay if you are okay."

"Well, I guess we are both okay, then."

Knowing his momma got nervous about his driving in the rain, Eddie had picked her up a copy of the *Times* to read as a distraction. As they headed to the corner, Eddie handed her the paper. Mother Mae returned a big smile and thanked him.

Soon, after exiting the interstate and proceeding down Main Street, Mother Mae looked up from her paper—just in time to see Pastor Walker's mother, Aretha Walker, get out of her big black Cadillac and head into the Main Street Fish Market.

Mother Mae pointed and shouted, "Eddie! Turn this truck around and take me to the fish market!"

Eddie said, "Yes, ma'am," and turned the truck into the parking lot of the post office, and then proceeded back down Main Street to the fish market. "Momma, what you need?"

Mother Mae shook her head. "Son, I just saw Pastor Walker's momma going into the fish market. It's important that I talk to her. There is something I need to know. We got to get to that fish market!"

"Okay, sure, Momma. We'll be there in a second, okay?"

Eddie pulled into Main Street Fish Market's parking lot and found a spot right up front by the entrance. After he parked and turned the truck off, he grabbed his momma's hand.

"Please don't get worked up about Pastor Walker. Promise me that we will leave if Pastor Walker's momma doesn't want to talk, okay?" He eyed her and tilted his head, waiting for her reply.

She sighed. "Okay, Eddie, I promise you I will not badger Aretha if she does not feel like speaking to me."

Mother Mae grabbed her purse and then Eddie helped her out of the truck. They entered the fish market and stood just inside the entrance looking around. Mother Mae spotted Aretha Walker making an order at the fresh-fish counter. Mother Mae moved quietly toward the spices and seasonings aisle, and stood in the cornmeal and fish-seasoning section to get a good view of Aretha. After Aretha retrieved her fish and began heading up front to check out, Mother Mae approached her.

"Oh my Lord, Aretha Walker! I am so glad to see you! How you doing?" Mother Mae asked, then gave her a big smile.

Aretha smiled back and replied, "Mother Mae, I am blessed."

As Aretha turned to leave, Mother Mae cleared her throat and said, "Aretha ... I was wondering, how is Pastor Walker?"

Aretha pursed her lips. "What was that?" she asked.

"We ... the mothers want to know. We are worried about him."

Aretha paused, turned around, cleared her throat, and said in a low voice, "Mother Mae, my son is going to be okay. Those devious and deceitful devils at One Way almost killed him, but God wouldn't allow it! One Way did my son wrong, and God is going to see to it that those trifling folks at One Way pay for it!"

Mother Mae could see the rage in Aretha's face, so she bowed her head and said, "I am so sorry, Aretha."

"Well," Aretha replied, "you tell them hypocritical deacons and that schizophrenic secretary to quit calling me and my family. We are tired of it! Just leave us alone. Mother Mae, those deacons and trustees are evil people, and if the congregation doesn't get a handle on things, those evildoers are going to destroy One Way."

Mother Mae just nodded.

With her bottom lip poked out, Aretha took her fish and headed to the next available cashier. Eddie quietly observed the whole ordeal from over in the produce section, and when he saw that his mother looked upset, he rushed to her and asked her if she was okay.

She replied, "I want to go home."

"Momma, don't you want me to take you to the store?"

"No, I don't feel so good." Her eyes welled with tears.

THE TRUTH

Mother Janie's telephone rang a total of ten times, but she refused to answer it. Mother Janie fussed that her family and friends all knew better than to be calling at 8:00 p.m. on Saturday night: "They know I watch *Cops* for the full hour and then I try to find *America's Most Wanted* at 9:00 p.m.," she muttered to herself.

The phone started to ring again, and now Mother Janie began to mumble about not having caller ID or voicemail. She wanted to ignore the call, but knew she couldn't, as it could be a true emergency.

She finally picked up the phone and shouted an unconvincing, "Praise the Lord!"

"Mother Janie, is that you?"

On the other end of the phone was Clara Mae James. Clara Mae, an off-and-on member of One Way for more than twenty years, only appeared at service when she was in trouble, needed a loan, or was grandstanding for her frequent out-of-town visitors. One Way never saw much of Clara Mae, and when they did, she was always bragging and shouting that she was the most committed member of the church. When she didn't get her way, she would threaten to move her membership, and she'd speak badly about the church to anyone that would listen.

Still irritated at the interruption, Mother Janie responded, "Who is this and what do you want?"

"Mother Janie, I am the one that should have an attitude since I have been calling for the last fifteen minutes. Why didn't you answer the phone?"

Mother Janie paused and quietly chanted "Jesus! Jesus! Jesus!" because something in Clara Mae's tone unsettled her.

Then, having recognized Clara Mae's infuriating voice, Mother Janie shouted back, "I don't know who you think you are talking to, but I am not one of your friends from the hood. When you find your manners, call me back!"

Mother Janie hung up the phone, grabbed her remote, and turned up the volume on her television. The phone began to ring again, and this time she answered with an even more insincere, "Praise the Lord!"

"Mother Janie, it's me, Clara Mae. How you doing?" she asked, sounding somewhat humbled and a bit more subdued.

"Baby, I am good. Now what do you need?"

"Mother Janie, why you think I need something? Can't I just be calling to see how you doing?"

"Yeah, you could, but you aren't, so what do you want?"

"Mother, my feelings are hurt."

Mother Janie rolled her eyes. "Clara Mae, in all the years I have known you, you have called me for gossip, money, meat, a ride, a gas can, sugar, flour, batteries, light bulbs, VCR tapes, Christmas wrapping paper, glue, stockings—look, you know I could go on for hours. Baby, what do you need?"

Clara Mae laughed and said, "Mother Janie, you know me so well."

"You got that right. So, sweetie, tell Mother what's going on."

"Mother Janie, my electricity is about to be shut off in forty-eight hours unless I come up with $600. Do you hear me? My babies and I are going to be cold and in the dark unless you give me $600."

"Well, Clara Mae, you will have to be cold and in the dark because I'm not giving you $600. Clara Mae, how did you run up a $600 bill? Child, that little house of yours is not even five hundred square feet."

"Mother, I mailed my payments in for the last three months, but the electric company told me yesterday they never received them." Her voice choked, but then she went on. "I can't find the receipts from the money orders, so I'm in a jam. Mother, we can't live in the dark and cold!"

Mother Janie held the phone away from her ear for a moment, shaking her head and rolling her eyes again. Then, while imitating the motion of someone playing a violin with her free hand, she pulled the phone back and responded, "Clara, you have been in the dark for many years, playing on the sympathy of One Way. It's time that you give your life to Jesus and let him provide for you. Stop all this foolishness and get right with the Lord."

"What? You did not say that! Why, I never!" Clara Mae said, then paused before taking a quieter tone. "Mother Janie, giving my life to Jesus today is not going to pay this $600 electric bill."

"But, baby, you will be at peace, and the Lord surely works in mysterious ways. Don't doubt him, and don't you dare mock him!"

Clara Mae gave a heavy sigh. "Mother Janie, please," she said, her words dripping with sweet honey.

"Uh-uh. Clara Mae, the babies you are talking about are over eighteen. Why aren't they working and helping you pay your $600 electric bill? I am sure their lazy behinds are using up most of the electricity. Why can't they help?"

Now Clara Mae grunted. "First of all, Mother Janie, that's none of your business, and secondly, you have no right to disrespect my children. For your information they are trying to find themselves."

Mother Janie held back a laugh. "Look here, Clara Mae. I have been patient with you and this sad story. Let me tell you something. No grown children are going to be lounging in my home, eating my food, coming and going as they please, and using my electric and water as they please if they are not contributing by working or going to school full-time. You have created this mess." She paused for a moment. "Huh. Finding themselves? They better find themselves a job!"

"Like I said before, Mother Janie, my kids are not your business. You talking crazy."

"Clara Mae, I am not going to tell you again to watch your mouth. I am not one of your girls. And another thing, I can't be too crazy, because my electricity has never, ever, ever been shut off. And one more thing: I was a working single parent to seven boys. All of my boys got jobs while they were in high school. Huh. So you definitely don't want to go there with me."

Another sigh from Clara Mae. "Forgive me, Mother Janie."

"I am sorry too, Clara Mae. You pushed and I pushed back. Look, bring your electric bill to church on Sunday morning, and I will ask the Mothers' Board to consider your request. If your request is granted, they will pay the electric company directly."

"No! Mother Janie, I need to take cash down to the electric company."

Sure you do, Mother Janie thought, but said, "If we agree to pay your bill, then we will take cash down to the electric company."

"Why won't you all just give me the money and let me handle it?"

"Clara Mae, to be frank, I just don't trust you. So giving you $600 is totally out of the question, but giving it directly to the electric company is a possibility. If I were in your shoes, I wouldn't care how the bill got paid, just as long as it got paid. Child, you need to get your priorities straight."

"Mother Janie," Clara Mae cried, "you aren't trying to help me; you don't even trust me. How is this going to look? What about my pride?"

"Baby, pride is what got you into this mess and you know what the Bible says: pride goes before destruction. Clara Mae, God loves you, One Way loves you, and I love you too. God bless you, and I pray we see you tomorrow for Sunday-morning service. Good night."

Mother Janie hung up the phone even as Clara Mae began pleading her case for the $600 cash loan. Mother Janie saw that she had missed the rest of *Cops.* "Hmph, figures!" she muttered, and then got ready for *America's Most Wanted*. This time she took the phone off the hook to avoid any further interruptions.

As Mother Janie went to the microwave to make some popcorn, she still felt plenty hot about how Clara Mae had the audacity to take her for a fool. *Girl must think I fell off some rickety turnip greens truck. She will not be calling me back tonight, and I certainly doubt that she will show up for service in the morning.*

On Sunday morning Clara Mae was indeed absent from church, but she had left a nasty message on the church answering machine asking for her membership to be terminated because she felt neglected and not a part of the family since neither the church nor the Mothers' Board would consider her request to borrow $600. She said that the church was not concerned about the poor and disabled, or the old and rich, but only the young and promising. She promised never again to step foot into One Way and said she hoped the church failed.

The Ushers' Board delivered this message in writing to Mother Janie, who read it and slipped it inside her Bible on the page of Proverbs 6, right between verses 9–19. They also delivered a copy of the message to Deacon Evans. Once he saw it was from Clara Mae, he stopped reading it any further and balled it up, then tossed it into the trash. Miss Lillian, the secretary, deleted the original voice message, and the call went unreturned.

Immediately after the service, the deacons and trustees called an emergency meeting and made the startling announcement that they were ready to conduct interviews for the vacant pastor position. Deacon Evans asked Lulabelle to come forward with the applicant pool information. Instead Frank Mason—member, church attorney, and nephew to Brother Ben—rushed forward to interrupt the meeting. He told Lulabelle to hold her seat and then asked the deacons to take their seats. Deacon Evans stood there, shaking his head, because he thought he was running the meeting, but he finally obliged out of fear because he had no clue as to what Brother Mason was about to reveal.

Brother Mason, pushing his glasses up on his nose, looked out on the congregation of about four hundred and said in a matter-of-fact way, "No new pastor will be interviewed, hired, or issued a contract without proper adherence to the church's bylaws on hiring a pastor. The church's bylaws were not followed, and I deem this meeting, and the process followed to date, unacceptable." Brother Mason waved the ushers up front. "Ushers, please come forward."

The ushers began to distribute to each member a copy of the church's bylaws for selecting a pastor, along with an attached list.

Deacon Evans' mouth dropped open.

Lulabelle nudged him in his arm and whispered, "What authority does he have to oversee this process?"

Deacon Evans glared at her and whispered, "Look behind you, woman! All those members will support him and give him the authority to enforce this charter."

Lulabelle's breath caught, then she reached into her briefcase for aspirin for her oncoming headache.

As Brother Mason continued, he began lecturing the congregation while moving from one aisle to another, explaining the church's bylaws. As he held up his index finger and looked directly at Deacon Evans and Lulabelle, he made the following statement:

"Members, no deacon, no trustee, and no member has the authority to independently engage in advertising, interviewing, and hiring a pastor. Please refer to page two of the bylaws: the eleven most senior members will make up the 'One Way Senior 11 Committee.' The One Way Senior 11 Committee will develop and agree on the timeline to hire, interview, and name a new pastor for One Way. When they meet, the entire congregation is allowed to come and observe the meetings. The entire congregation is able to vote on the two finalists whom the One Way Senior 11 Committee presents as the top two candidates. No contract will be issued without the strict adherence to our charter, and we will not deviate from this whatsoever. One Way, do you understand what I have explained to you? Please say 'Amen.'"

The church responded in unison with a firm "Amen."

"Any questions?" Brother Mason asked as he looked over the congregation.

Mother Janie stood and asked, "Who are the One Way Senior 11 Committee members?'"

Brother Mason nodded at her. "Great question, Mother Janie. Miss Lillian and I came up with the list, and it is on the attached blue sheet of paper. I will read the names aloud. The eleven most senior active members of One Way are the following: Mother Mae, Mother Janie, Mother Kellie, Mother Addie, Mother Millie, Lulabelle Evans, Deacon Evans, Deacon King, Deacon Carter, Usher Gibson, and Evangelist Hattie. Because Mother Mae is the most senior member of the committee, she has been identified as the committee chairwoman."

He nodded to Mother Janie again, and she sat down.

"Members," he went on, "I have nothing further to address. If you don't have any questions for me, then I will take my seat."

The members sat quietly as Brother Mason headed to his seat, but then, before he reached it, the congregation responded with a round of applause. He smiled and sat down next to his uncle, Brother Ben.

A proud Brother Ben shook his hand and told him, "Nephew, you did an awesome job."

"Thanks, Uncle Ben, but I know there are going to be some members who are going to test the waters and see what they can get away with."

"Nephew, now who would be foolish enough to even think they have the power to challenge the rules established by this church so many years ago?"

Brother Mason gave a sly smile. "Deacon and Sister Evans do. In fact they believe they have more power than any other member of One Way."

"Nephew, this is news to me. How is it that they are able to exude so much power over a large congregation?"

Now Brother Mason shrugged. "They read everything, and are Bible smart. They're involved in all aspects of the church, they tend to have a hand in everything that goes on at One Way because of the positions they have, and they are not shy about it. The only folks they tend to back down from are the mothers. The mothers hold the history and knowledge about One Way; the mothers have direct influence over more than 80 percent of the membership. This is where the conflict arises, because the mothers can't be challenged on any rules or history regarding the church. Furthermore, the mothers are serious tithers and dues-paying members. The checking, savings, and money market accounts of the Mothers' Board are not managed by the trustees. They have their own private accountant. Of course, this nags the Evanses to no end. They have tried more than several times to dismantle the Mothers' Board, but they can't get the support."

"Hmm, interesting," replied Uncle Ben. "Perhaps I should pay more attention to the goings-on at this church."

Brother Mason frowned and looked at the floor. "Maybe everyone should."

FALLEN SOLDIER

Another hardship suddenly unfolded within the One Way church family when word spread regarding the passing of One Way's eldest deacon, Deacon Roscoe Morgan. Deacon Morgan had been called to heaven after a lengthy illness. Before taking ill, Deacon Morgan had kept a perfect attendance record at the church. The ninety-one-year-old deacon had been a member at One Way for more than sixty years. Until about three months ago the church deacons had delivered communion to Deacon Morgan at his home. Once word got back to the Trustee Board that Deacon Morgan had stopped sending his tithes and stopped paying his deacon membership dues during his illness, the trustees placed his membership on probation, cut him off from communion, and revoked his title as deacon.

His daughter, Faye, also a member of One Way, had explained to Deacon Evans that they could no longer afford to keep sending her father's tithes and membership dues, and still pay for his medicine. Deacon Evans had assured Faye that One Way understood. Then he sent a short and nasty letter via certified mail on church stationery advising Faye that Deacon Morgan's inability to pay his tithes and membership to the church was a personal problem and not the church's problem. The letter included a full accounting of the past due amount owed to One Way. Devastated, Faye could only shake her head over the church's position after all the years of service her father had given to One Way.

Now, after her father's passing, Faye struggled with her faith in God—and in One Way. But then she remembered how, during her father's illness, some members would call, write, or drop by to see about her father. Those memories brought tears to her eyes and gave her hope that the entire church had not abandoned her during this difficult time. She then remembered how the Mothers' Board and Missionary Board would deliver cooked meals and stay for hours chatting with her father.

"Oh, how my father loved One Way," she whispered, trying to outweigh the bad with the good.

Faye let her mind wander back to some of the wonderful moments her father had shared with the Mothers' Board. She recalled that when the deacons had refused to deliver communion to her father, the Mothers' Board had picked up where the deacons left off. It appeared that her father had enjoyed it even more after the deacons stopped participating. The mothers would sit and laugh with her father and tell stories from the old days that would set the entire room into laughter. But when it was time for prayer, tears and shouts of joy would illuminate any darkened soul in the room.

The mothers treated Faye like their own daughter. They knew she had a hard burden caring for her father and her small children. Faye was the light of Deacon Morgan's life, a daddy's girl in every sense. The love she had for her father was immeasurable. So it came as no shock to anyone when Faye had uprooted her kids, sold her house, and taken off from Atlanta to move to One Way to be with her father when he'd fallen ill.

That night Faye fell asleep crying, both tears of sadness and of joy.

The next morning the mothers called Deacon King to drive them to Deacon Morgan's home so they could pay their respects and deliver the food they had prepared for the family. The mothers believed home-cooked food was perceived as a source of nourishment and comfort to the bereaved during their time of loss, disappointment, and pain. So they always took extra care when preparing and delivering food during times of sorrow. As they got closer to Deacon Morgan's home, they all talked about how great a daughter and mother Faye measured up to be, and they also shared fond memories about Deacon Morgan. As they approached the railroad tracks near Deacon Morgan's home, they looked down the street and saw cars packed in the driveway in front of the redbrick home. Visitors came and went, with the white screen door of the one-story home constantly swinging open and slamming shut. The mothers knew that many family members of Deacon Morgan had arrived to help prepare for the funeral.

But then they spotted Deacon Evans' big Lincoln Town Car blocking the front of the driveway.

"What are they doing here?" Mother Janie asked as she pointed at the car.

Mother Kellie replied, "Probably in there stealing from the dead."

As the mothers descended from the van, Deacon King opened the rear doors, pulled out the utility cart, and proceeded to unload boxes of fried chicken, potato salad, macaroni and cheese, collard greens, cornbread, cakes, pies, and sodas.

"Mmm-mm!" Deacon King said. "Mothers, this food is sure smelling good. Deacon Morgan's family will be happy to feast on this."

The mothers replied in near unison, "Thank you, Deacon King."

As the mothers walked to the doorstep, they could hear Lulabelle inside, shouting, "I could care less about feelings. I have the final say on this matter, and if you don't like it, you can kiss my @#$!"

Lulabelle flung open the front door as she said the last word—and got a surprise upon seeing the mothers standing on the other side of the screen door. Her eyes wide, Lulabelle began sweating and rushed to get out the door.

But Deacon Miller caught Lulabelle by the arm and said, "How dare you speak to this family in such a nasty manner! Deacon Morgan was my mentor, our church's eldest deacon—show this family some respect."

"Mind your business, Larry!" Lulabelle shouted. She jerked her arm away from his grasp and pushed open the screen door. "Praise the Lord, Mothers!" she shouted.

The mothers stood there, frozen by what they had just witnessed. Some gave Lulabelle evil glares, while others mumbled "I declare" or "That just isn't right" or the like.

Lulabelle emerged and muttered "Excuse me, excuse me" as all the mothers stood like statutes to force Lulabelle to go around all of them.

Once Lulabelle had huffed off, the mothers entered the home. They found Faye in tears, with other family members shaking their heads and speaking in hushed tones to comfort one another.

Feeling a stirring in her soul, Mother Kellie whispered to all the other mothers, "Let's praise the Lord with 'We've Come This Far by Faith.'"

The mothers all nodded, and the song began. Singing the song lifted the darkness from the room, like a fresh wind blowing away a dense fog. Everyone joined in. Folks clapped, tapped their feet, smiled at each other, and held hands. When the song ended, the mothers prayed for the family. Finally they presented Faye with a check for $500—and all the wonderful home-cooked food they had prepared.

As the mothers set up the food in the kitchen, Faye pulled Mother Mae aside and told her that the family had decided to have only graveside services tomorrow for Deacon Morgan.

"Faye," Mother Mae said, "your father would want to have his service at One Way, and One Way would be honored to send Deacon Morgan off with a soul-stirring home-going celebration."

"Mother Mae, I know, but we don't want any big fuss. We just want to bury Daddy as soon as possible. You know Daddy was a simple man."

Mother Mae nodded. "I have to respect your wishes, but I know for a fact he would have wanted his home-going celebration held at his church."

Faye gave a tight smile and nodded. "I know. I know that, Mother Mae, I do. But we decided to put Daddy to rest as soon as possible without too much fanfare. I hope I can count on you and the mothers to be there."

Mother Mae reached out put a hand on Faye's left forearm. "Sure will, baby. All of us will be there to make sure our brother is sent off in praise and celebration. We will honor your wishes, and you know to call if you need us."

Faye grabbed hold of Mother Mae and hugged her as both had tears streaming from their eyes.

Mother Mae then took Faye by the hand and led her back into the kitchen. "Baby," she said, "get you a plate and get something to eat."

"Yes, ma'am," Faye said. Then she wiped her nose with a wad of tissue someone had quietly slipped her.

The kitchen was full of folks eating, laughing, and just looking around. Deacon Morgan had a huge country kitchen with a fireplace in it. Chairs sat here and there and everywhere as folks dug into the various dishes and then took a seat to enjoy the soul food prepared by the mothers. Deacon King just couldn't help himself. He looked a mess sitting there, with crumbs, hot sauce, and mustard splotched all over his shirt. It seemed as if he hadn't eaten in years.

Finally, as Deacon King got up for more, Mother Kellie told him, "Deacon King, you are eating like a wild animal. Now calm down and let the entire family eat before you go back for seconds."

Deacon King nodded, gave a sheepish little smile, and then returned to his seat.

A little while later, the mothers began packing up what they could and making their way out to their van. Each mother stopped to hug Faye on the way out. As the mothers loaded onto the van, Deacon King told them they had outdone themselves again. They all blushed and thanked him.

Before Deacon King even got to the second streetlight past Deacon Morgan's home, the mothers were snoring up a storm. Deacon King chuckled to himself, knowing this was a sure sign that the mothers felt at peace with what they had done. If they had been dissatisfied, Deacon King would have been enduring loud discussions, emotional eruptions, and general handwringing during the ride home.

THE FUNERAL

On the sunny morning of Deacon Morgan's funeral, his family and friends gathered under a green tent at Morning Glory Cemetery, facing a beautiful black casket with brushed nickel-colored accents. Faye made sure the mothers had a row of seats right behind the family. Once everyone had gotten settled, Minister Pate, the cemetery's on-call minister, called for the One Way Church resolution to be read, and everyone began looking around to see who would come forward. Then, from the rear, Lulabelle came striding forward in a striking—and inappropriate—red suit, red hat, and, yes, matching red shoes. Before Lulabelle could get to the podium, Faye stood up and tapped Lulabelle on her shoulder, stopping her in her tracks.

Looking straight into Lulabelle's eyes, Faye said in a soft but firm tone, "My family would want Daddy's resolution to be read by someone who actually loved him, like Mother Mae."

Lulabelle gave a choked breath, then let her mouth hang open as she just glared at Faye. Then Lulabelle glanced at Minister Pate, but before she could speak, the minister twitched his nose and shook his head from side to side as he pointed Lulabelle back to her seat. Then Minister Pate waved Mother Mae up front. Mother Mae made her way up front and greeted Lulabelle. As Mother Mae reached out for the resolution, Lulabelle dropped the resolution to the ground. Miss

Lillian, sitting nearby, quickly stooped down, picked up the resolution, and handed it to Mother Mae.

Minister Pate looked ready to chew nails, so he called out to Lulabelle, "Excuse me, ma'am—you in the red suit!"

Lulabelle stopped and whirled around, her jaw clenched and her eyes like ice.

"There is no place for ungodliness at this home-going celebration," Minister Pate called out. "Please come back and retrieve the resolution from Miss Lillian, and place it in the hands of Mother Mae. Before I allow you to disrespect Deacon Morgan, this grieving family, and Mother Mae, I will have you escorted out of here. Now … let's try this again."

Biting her bottom lip, Lulabelle returned and gently took the resolution from Miss Lillian, then shoved it into the hands of Mother Mae while giving her a scowl. The entire congregation rose to their feet and applauded Minister Pate. Steaming, Lulabelle turned to head back to her seat—and tripped over Deacon King's foot, falling into his lap. Laughter erupted from the rear of the tent as Deacon King attempted to assist Lulabelle up from his lap.

Taking a breath to calm herself, Mother Mae made her way up front. She pulled her reading glasses from her pocket once she arrived at the podium and then unfolded the resolution.

As she glanced over the typewritten page, Mother Mae kept thinking about how proud Deacon Morgan was when Pastor Walker became One Way's new pastor. She recalled him telling the mothers during one of their after-church dinners at the local Soul Food Buffet that he would just die of a broken heart if One Way lost Pastor Walker over some foolishness.

Clearing her throat, Mother Mae pulled herself together and began reading the resolution: "'At the gates of heaven, the Lord said to Deacon Morgan, "Well done, thou good and faithful servant: thou hast been faithful over a few things. I will make thee ruler over many things: enter thou into the joy of the Lord."'"

"'We come today to celebrate the life of our beloved and faithful friend, Deacon Roscoe Morgan, who has now found rest in the arm of Jesus. Deacon Morgan served One Way faithfully for more than sixty years as chairman of the deacons, devoted Sunday school teacher, male chorus member, and church plumber.'"

Mother Mae paused and looked at the family, then continued. "'To the family, lean not to your own understanding but seek and trust God. He will see each one of you through it all. One Way extends its sincere sympathy and …'"

Now Mother Mae choked up and felt tears in her eyes. When the other mothers saw her pausing and noticed her hands trembling, they encouraged her by calling out, "Take your time," and "Mother Mae, no need in rushing."

Mother Mae gave a smile through her tears, then went on and finished reading the resolution: "'One Way extends its sincere sympathy and will be ardently praying for you. Be it resolved that we accept what God has done, knowing that all things work together for the good of them that love God. Our Lord promised to never fail you, and he will guide you through it all. Be if further resolved that he knows your pain and he will be your strength; further resolved that a copy of this resolution be given to the family of Deacon Roscoe Morgan and a copy be filed in our church records this day. Humbly and prayerfully submitted by the membership of One Way Missionary Baptist Church.'" She looked up and said, "Thank you."

As Mother Mae wiped tears from her eyes, Faye walked up to the podium and hugged her.

"Thank you, Mother Mae," she whispered. "Daddy would have been proud."

With tears still in her eyes, Mother Mae walked slowly back to her seat among the mothers. On his way back to the podium, Minister Pate commended Mother Mae on a job well done. And when Mother Mae took her seat, the other mothers patted her on her back and whispered "Good job" and similar praise.

Minister Pate introduced the soloist. Out of the corner of her eye, though, Mother Mae saw Lulabelle giving her a glare. But Mother Mae just kept facing forward, then smiled and nodded as the soloist began to sing "Amazing Grace."

Mother Mae leaned to her right and whispered to Mother Janie, "How can a song like 'Amazing Grace' not make you want to cry? It has such a powerful meaning, no matter who sings it. Oh, it hits me so hard."

"It's going to be okay, Mother Mae," Mother Janie whispered back.

As the beautiful notes faded into silence, for some reason Mother Mae's mind drifted back to Pastor Walker. She recalled how Lulabelle and Deacon Evans treated Deacon Morgan so cruelly after Pastor Walker's installation as One Way's new pastor. She remembered the phone calls from Deacon Morgan asking her to pray with him after Deacon Evans made one of his many belittling comments. She just couldn't shake her suspicion that Lulabelle and Deacon Evans might have had something to do with Pastor Walker's abrupt departure, especially since they seemed to be in such a rush to get a new pastor.

Hmm … could this have more significance than I realize?

Thoughts like that kept coming and going, but then Minister Pate's eulogy brought Mother Mae right back to the present. His powerful and heartfelt words brought the seated folks to their feet.

As Deacon Morgan's casket was lowered into the ground, Faye's shrieking cries sent chills throughout the people in the tent. Faye had told the mothers during one of their visits that she never attended a funeral without reliving the grief of her mother's death, and she believed burying her father would be even more traumatic.

The funeral home director addressed the crowd and instructed the family to return to the limousines. From there the family would return to Deacon Morgan's home.

The mothers assembled on the church van and waved as they passed the family car. The mood on the van started out somber, but Mother Janie spiced it up by saying, "Minister Pate sure got Lulabelle told, didn't he?"

Then the other mothers jumped in saying, "Wasn't the look on her face priceless?" and "Someone should have taken a picture!"

"Ha! Deacon Morgan is probably still laughing," Mother Kellie said. "Oh, and Mother Mae sure did a good job reading that resolution, didn't she? I don't think I could have pulled it off."

All the mothers offered their agreement that Mother Mae did indeed do a fine job.

"Well," Mother Mae said, "I just wanted to make Faye and Deacon Morgan proud."

From the front of the bus, Deacon King looked in the rearview mirror and said, "You did well, Mother Mae. They had to be pleased."

Mother Mae thanked him for his kind words, and then Mother Janie then jumped in: "Deacon King, how 'bout it? Did you deliberately trip Lulabelle or was it really an accident?"

Deacon King snorted a laugh, then responded, "Mother Janie, that woman was so mad that she didn't see anything but self-importance, and she just stumbled on my foot. That is the Lord's truth, and I'm sticking to it!"

The mothers belted out so much laughter that Deacon King had to focus on his driving—because he was about ready to fall out of his seat from laughing so hard himself.

ANOTHER FUNERAL

The day after Deacon Morgan's funeral, Evangelist Hattie kept trying to reach Mothers Janie, Mae, and Millie, because she had received a last-minute request to officiate at a local gang member's funeral on the west side, at the Down Under Funeral Home—a place located in an area well known for its gang activity and shootings.

Once Evangelist Hattie got through to Mothers Mae, Janie, and Millie, she begged each of the mothers to accompany her to a funeral. After hearing the request individually, the three of them got together and debated the idea. Finally the mothers halfheartedly decided that they all would go to support Evangelist Hattie.

After the decision was made and they all went their separate ways, though, Mother Millie began to have second thoughts about the wisdom of their decision. So, once home, she made a three-way call to Mothers Janie and Mae, and expressed her concerns about going to that side of town—the same concerns she had brought up when they'd met to talk about it. She reminded them—again—that this was a gang member's funeral and the crowd it would attract would not include many upstanding citizens. More importantly, she said, Evangelist Hattie's frightening driving skills would be a real threat to their safety.

Affectionately known to everyone as "Evangelist Hattie," Hattie Jackson-Bailey-Brown had been a permanent fixture at One Way for more than forty years. One Way members learned long ago not to ask Evangelist Hattie how she was feeling. She was known to tell whoever asked that her arthritis was acting up, her gout had gotten her down, her back was so bent out of shape that she hadn't slept in days, and her migraines were keeping her vision so cloudy that she could barely see.

Further, even with the drums positioned right behind her pulpit chair, somehow Evangelist Hattie could manage to throw her head back and fall soundly asleep and not be moved by the beat of the drums during a service. Several times an usher had been forced to shake her because she had gotten so comfortable that she had pulled her hat, wig, and shoes off right before the congregation, all while sound asleep.

Not unexpectedly, Evangelist Hattie's driving skills were nonexistent. She had knocked down One Way's street sign several times. Twice in the last three months, Evangelist Hattie had run into and dragged the church mailbox more than twenty feet, and last year she ran over Deacon Evans' foot when he was guiding her into a tight parking space. After he hollered and acted a fool, pleading for her to get off his foot, she backed up and ran over his other foot. Evangelist Hattie felt bad about the incident and paid all of Deacon Evans' medical bills, but he and Lulabelle never forgave her.

Evangelist Hattie's first two husbands died of heart attacks while she was driving them to doctors' appointments. She claimed the heart attacks had nothing to do with her driving skills, but members of One Way knew enough not to ride with her. Hence, it was truly understandable that Mother Millie felt concerned about traveling with Evangelist Hattie. Mothers Mae and Janie argued that Evangelist Hattie hadn't had a serious accident in a very long time, and that the mothers should support Evangelist Hattie on her first funeral eulogy. Though reluctant, Mother Millie finally agreed.

The day came and the mothers traveled with Evangelist Hattie to the Down Under Funeral Home. As Evangelist Hattie drove them in her white conversion van with dark tinted windows, anyone watching from the sidewalk would have thought the devil sat behind the wheel. At one point the van jerked to the right and swerved up onto a curve, into some shrubs, and then back onto the road. The mothers just held on for dear life, praying, screaming, and crying.

After the ten-mile trip, the mothers felt exhausted and edgy. After looking for hats, shoes, purses, and jewelry that had come loose during the ride, they finally pulled themselves together and calmed down as they entered the small, windowless black building that served as a bingo hall on Thursday and Saturday nights and a funeral home the rest of the time. The building sat right next to the riverbank in West One Way.

Before entering, Mother Janie whispered to Mother Addie, "I wonder how many bodies and cars are sitting at the bottom of that river? I bet this funeral home has dumped its share of bodies in there too."

Fixing her hat, Mother Addie said, "Mother Janie, let's keep the focus on Jesus and the bereaved family, and less on crime."

"Sure, sweetie," Mother Janie said as she held the door open for Mother Addie.

It was hard for the mothers to blend in, as they were the only silver-haired women in the audience. The funeral home was able to seat around seventy-five people, and it was filled to capacity. All the faces looked young—and rough. Rows of chairs faced the casket and podium. As the mothers gathered up front to view the body of this young man who was killed as a result of gun violence, they each said a brief prayer over him before moving to greet the family. When Mother Addie stepped up to view the body, her hat hit the digital bingo sign hanging over the coffin. The sign flashed *B5* in a fire-engine-red color. After Mother Addie prayed and lifted her head up, the sign flashed *WINNER* and the sirens went off, startling the family and friends. An embarrassed Mother Addie took her hat off as she continued down the line.

As the funeral home staff tried to turn off the sign, Bobby Womack's "If You Think You're Lonely Now" blared over the speakers for all of thirty seconds. Finally the lights above the coffin shut off and soft music began playing again.

As soon as Mother Millie arrived at the casket, she began to scream and holler. She dropped to her knees and began to cry uncontrollably. Mother Addie turned back to go help her. Mother Addie stooped down to the floor, wrapped her arms around Mother Millie's back, and whispered, "Millie, you okay? Calm down now. Let's get up, because there are people waiting in line to view the body. Okay?"

As Mother Millie regained her composure, she looked up at Mother Addie and said, "Evangelist Hattie's driving really got to me. I have never been so afraid in my life. I guess this has been building up ever since we got the invitation, and then her driving this morning must have put me over the edge."

Then she lost it again and began to sob. Her cries led others to cry, and everyone soon seemed out of control. Mother Addie held Mother Millie's arm, and they took their seats with the other mothers. By the time Mother Millie sat down, she smiled at Mother Addie.

Then Mother Millie leaned over with a puzzled look on her face. "Did I start all this crying?" she asked Mother Addie.

Trying not to laugh, Mother Addie answered, "You betcha!"

As the mothers got settled in their seats on the opposite side of the family, they began to feel agitated by a surge of heat gushing from the ceiling vents.

Fanning herself with a hand, Mother Mae clucked her tongue, then asked, "What kind of mess did Evangelist Hattie get us into? She knows this kind of heat gets my blood pressure up."

The mothers stripped off their jackets, and all of them began a mad flurry of fanning, some with their hands and some with small hand fans pulled from the purses. As Evangelist Hattie came forward to eulogize the young man before his unsaved family and friends, Mother Mae fanned herself with two hand fans and belted out, "Father, Father, please Father, let there be some cool air somewhere."

Mother Janie shouted, "Amen!"

Evangelist Hattie heard only the "Amen" from Mother Janie and figured that was her cue to move the service along, so she shouted, "Don't let this young man's life be in vain! Stand up for Jesus! Stand up for God! Stand up for Jehovah! Folks, we got to stand for something. Why don't you get up out of your seats and stand for something that's good for you. Something that can save your life, your family, your children! Somebody better get up and stand with me. I know it's hot up in here, but if you don't get this life down here right, you will experience hotter temperatures down there." As Evangelist Hattie pointed down to the floor, the room fell quiet. She, in turn, became quiet and prayed to the Lord as sweat poured from her. Closing her eulogy, she began to sing "Near the Cross."

"Help me sing folks!" she said.

Of course the only folks who could help her with the song were the mothers, but they were too hot to keep the song going. As the funeral home staff came forward to shut the casket, moans and cries emanated from the crowd. Since the family had opted for cremation, the service ended after the body was removed.

The mothers stood outside, next to Evangelist Hattie's conversion van, as they waited for her to depart the funeral home. Mother Millie began to tear up again as she saw all the scrapes, dents, and dings on the van. She whispered, "Had I seen all of this when Hattie stopped by to pick me up, I would have never got in. I would have stayed home. That woman just can't drive. Sweet as pie, but can't drive. You saw how she kept turning around from her seat to talk to us when she was driving us here? You saw how she was text-messaging and driving? I know you saw how she put cream and sugar in her coffee and stirred it—while driving! We almost hit the school crossing guard back on Vernon, and she clipped that milk truck and kept going. And don't even get me started about her smashing up those shrubs! Call me paranoid, but Hattie should have had her license revoked years ago. How could they keep renewing her license year after year?"

"Now come on," Mother Addie said, "you know that Evangelist Hattie's stepson works down at the DMV. We all know what he is doing."

With tears now streaming down her face, Mother Millie began sobbing. "I can't do it! I can't get back in this van."

Mother Janie grabbed her cousin by the arm and said, "Millie, pull yourself together. Just close your eyes and pray like the rest of us. Okay?"

Mother Millie sniffled and gave a little nod. "I'll try!"

"Your sobs, screaming, and speaking in tongues during the ride are not helpful to the rest of us either," Mother Janie said. "Do you really think we enjoy hitting curb after curb, having our purses and Bibles thrown from seat to seat when she turns on two wheels? We don't, but we made a promise to be there for each other. Can you do that much for me?"

Still sniffling and wiping her eyes, Mother Millie said, "Janie, I'm going to do my best. I'll just close my eyes and pray. Thank you, cousin."

Mother Janie hugged Mother Millie and said, "You know I got your back. When you think about it, it's not that bad; it's not even ten miles."

They both shared a nervous laugh as they saw Evangelist Hattie come out the building.

"Mothers," Evangelist Hattie called out as she approached. "Gather 'round. I have something important to share with you about Pastor Walker's disappearance. Please gather around."

With whispers and murmurs, the mothers hurried to huddle around Evangelist Hattie and hear her news.

"Mothers, I have been praying and fasting for answers regarding Pastor Walker," Evangelist Hattie said. "The Spirit of the Lord finally spoke to me."

Mother Janie sighed and shook her head. "Oh, really? And what exactly did the Spirit say?"

Evangelist Hattie peered at her through slit eyelids. "Mother Janie, do I detect sarcasm?"

"Oh my no. Not at all, Hattie. We have been so anxious to hear some news. I know the Lord has used you many times before to prophesy to One Way. So please, share." Mother Janie touched Evangelist Hattie's shoulder and nodded for her to continue.

"Thank you. Well, it has been revealed to me by the Spirit of the Lord that Pastor Walker is in confinement. The Spirit has assured me that although Pastor Walker is in confinement, he is not in danger."

"What? Confinement?" Mother Janie said. "You mean like in the hospital or locked in a basement or attic in captivity?"

"Or she could mean on lockdown at a mental hospital," Mother Millie said.

Evangelist Hattie shook her head. "Mothers, this is all the Spirit has revealed to me. If more information or clarification is revealed, I will share it. Mothers, we need to get going." With that she walked toward the driver's door of her van.

Mother Mae had apparently had a "revelation" too, because she cleared her throat and announced to Evangelist Hattie that the mothers had an urgent business matter to attend to and Deacon King would be picking them up. She thanked Evangelist Hattie for the opportunity to support her during the eulogy for the young man's home-going celebration. She reiterated that Evangelist Hattie would always have the mothers' love and support for future engagements. The mothers then all waved good-bye and exhaled a sigh of relief as Evangelist drove out of the parking lot.

Mother Mae pulled out her phone and called Deacon King to come pick them up, then looked at all the mothers and said, "I just felt like we maybe had enough fellowship time with her today, don't you think?"

"Oh, thank you, Lord!" Mother Millie said. "Hallelujah! And thank you Mother Mae for godly wisdom!"

"Amen," Mother Kellie said. "Now, Mother Mae, what do you make of Evangelist Hattie's revelation?"

"Mothers, I believe in the power of the Holy Spirit," Mother Mae said. "If Evangelist Hattie said the Lord revealed to her that our pastor is in confinement, then I believe it. If you don't believe it, pray and ask God for an answer."

Whispers of "Amen" and nods of approval came from the mothers—along with prayers for Evangelist Hattie's trip back to her house and plenty more thanksgiving that Deacon King would be driving them home.

FESTIVAL PLANNING

Even though the majority of the congregation had little to no interest in planning the church's annual fall festival, Lulabelle felt just thrilled to be involved in planning another great festival. The mayhem brewing over the replacement of Pastor Walker didn't affect Lulabelle's desire to outdo all of the members by lavishly spending for the festival—and then taking all the credit. In truth the majority of the members felt the festival should be cancelled in light of recent circumstances.

In addition to Lulabelle, Miss Lillian, Mother Kellie, Brother Luther Dixon, and Sister Melody Note had been organizers of the church festival since its inception in 1995. Lulabelle demanded the first planning meeting be held at her house—so that she would not have to drive and park her brand-new Cadillac in questionable neighborhoods for meetings at the houses of the other organizers. Of course, the rest of the committee resented this demand but felt obliged ... and this would be a once-in-a-lifetime opportunity to get a glimpse of the exquisite home of Lulabelle and Deacon Evans.

On Tuesday evening, twenty minutes prior to 6:00 p.m., Mother Kellie rolled up in her sleek new black Corvette with Sister Melody Note in the passenger seat. Ten minutes later Miss Lillian, in her 1971 white Cadillac Coupe de Ville, raced down the quiet, neatly manicured street at more than fifty miles per hour, with a thunderous sound and smoke emitting from the rear of her vehicle, passing houses that could easily sell for half a million dollars. Soon enough Miss Lillian, who could barely see over the steering wheel, navigated the big Cadillac into Lulabelle's driveway—and totally misjudged it, scraping Lulabelle's mailbox. As a result the mailbox was bent to the left, but amazingly Miss Lillian's Cadillac suffered no visible damage. As she backed away from the mailbox, Miss Lillian jumped the curb and ended up on the Evans' lawn. Finally she just pulled up and parked at an angle, which blocked in Mother Kellie and Lulabelle's vehicles.

Rushing from her vehicle to be punctual, Miss Lillian hit the alarm button on her keychain remote and then proceeded to the entrance of the Evans' home. After touching the doorbell, Deacon Evans opened the tall cherry-wood door and invited Miss Lillian into his home. While holding the door open and motioning for Miss Lillian to come in, Deacon Evans slit his eyes at Miss Lillian and said, "I hope that big limousine of yours is not leaking oil in my driveway, cause if it is, I will send you a bill to have it cleaned up."

Miss Lillian ignored him and walked through the huge foyer that housed a gigantic grandfather clock, a massive oak console table, and a mirror. Just as she approached the living room, she heard Deacon Evans yell, "Hold up, Miss Lillian!"

Miss Lillian stopped and turned around, then calmly asked, "Now what?"

"This is not the ghetto or projects. You could have parked that hearse better than that."

Miss Lillian looked at him. "I just love you, Deacon Evans. Now where is the powder room?"

A befuddled-looking Deacon Evans shook his head, "Jesus, give me patience to get through the night. Please, Jesus," he mumbled under his breath as he pointed Miss Lillian to the restroom.

Before Deacon Evans could get into the kitchen to finish preparing snacks, he got distracted by loud, booming music coming from the street. As he glanced out of the sidelight from his foyer, he saw Brother Luther Dixon bobbing his head to music overshadowed by the bass, which resulted in Deacon Evans' front door vibrating. Deacon Evans opened the door and tried unsuccessfully to get Luther's attention. Sitting in his classic 1969 black Chevrolet Nova convertible with dual exhaust pipes and spinning rims, Luther kept bobbing to his hard-core rap music.

Now steaming mad, Deacon Evans ran from his front door, down the lawn, and shouted, "Where do you think you are? Turn that crap off! This is not that type of neighborhood."

Brother Luther nodded twice and flashed the peace sign to Deacon Evans as he turned the music down and raised the convertible top on his car. As Luther got out of his car, he hit his alarm button and said to Deacon Evans, "You tripping if you think your neighbors don't like a little rap music."

Deacon Evans just stared at Luther. "Man, look around you! None of your homeboys live in this neighborhood. Show some respect!" He paused, then shouted, "And get off my grass! Man, you trying my patience."

Smiling and bobbing to the music in his head, Luther followed Deacon Evans into the house.

As Miss Lillian exited the powder room, she greeted Luther just as he entered into the formal sunken living room. Their eyes lit up like children in a toy store.

"My, oh my, Lulabelle," Miss Lillian said. "What a beautiful home you have here. The Lord has truly blessed you and Deacon Evans. Oh my goodness, is this a Persian rug?"

"Yes, it is, Miss Lillian," Lulabelle said. Then, with her finger raised in the air, Lulabelle announced, "Before you and Luther step on it, please remove your shoes."

"Oh, um, of course," Miss Lillian said.

After she and Luther removed their shoes, they made their way over to Lulabelle's sumptuous Italian leather sofa, where Mother Kellie and Sister Melody already sat. The sofa had a camel back so high that you couldn't see Luther's, Miss Lillian's, Sister Melody's, or Mother Kellie's head from behind.

Once they got seated, all eyes went to Luther's stinky bare feet. With her nose turned up, Lulabelle gave Luther a "How dare you" stare. Luther nodded at her as if nothing were wrong.

Mother Kellie squeezed Miss Lillian's hand, saying, "Good to see you, Miss Lillian."

"It's good to see you too, Mother Kellie. How are you doing, Melody?"

"I'm good, Miss Lillian," mumbled Melody as she texted up a storm, waiting for the meeting to convene.

Lulabelle excused herself from the living room to bring in refreshments, grinning at the ladies as she exited the room.

Mother Kellie whispered, "Lulabelle sure has exquisite taste."

"And plenty of money to support it," Melody said.

With her legs crossed and exposing holes in her clean white socks, Miss Lillian whispered, "Money can't buy you happiness—or self-respect. The occupants of this home are lacking both, and are evildoers. Don't be fooled by these riches and false idols. If anyone should know, I would."

Mother Kellie and Melody glanced at each other, and Melody shrugged her shoulders. Meanwhile Luther, sitting relaxed on the sofa, began to doze off and snore.

As Lulabelle returned, she announced, "Refreshments are served." She brought in a sterling-silver tray and coffee set while Deacon Evans rolled up a serving cart, which featured a sterling-silver punch bowl and a tray of finger sandwiches, a tray of assorted cakes, and a tray of fruit and cheese. The ladies "Oo-ed" and "Ahh-ed" at the beautiful serving dishes displayed on the cart.

As Deacon Evans picked up the cart and carried it down into the living room, he stopped and shouted, "Whew, where is that foul odor coming from?"

Everyone looked at Luther, who was now loudly snoring in a deep sleep. Deacon Evans pushed Luther's shoulder and shouted for him to wake up.

Luther jumped, with slobber running from his face onto the sofa, and asked, "What's up, dude?"

Deacon Evans asked Luther to come with him and to bring his shoes. Deacon Evans took Luther back to a guest bedroom and told him to have a seat. Luther looked into the vanity table mirror and gathered himself together. Soon Deacon Evans reappeared with a can of Foot Magic Spray and a pair of socks.

"Here, man, spray this on your feet and in those funky shoes. You could have brought some funky fungus into my home. Now I am going to have to get that rug cleaned. You want to be cool, buy you some socks and shoes."

Still half-asleep, Luther took the spray and socks. "Deacon Evans, thank you."

"Yeah, just do me one favor."

"You name it and I'll do it," Luther said.

"Forget my address. Don't ever come back to my house, understood?"

Luther nodded. "Deacon Evans, I am a man of my word. I will never ever come back to your house," he said as he put on the white athletic socks. Then he and Deacon Evans returned to the living room with his odor-free shoes.

"Now that Luther is back, we can now get this meeting moving," Lulabelle said.

Mother Kellie spoke up: "Before you go any further, Lulabelle, we would like to vote on postponing the church festival until further notice. We feel it would be in the best interest of the church membership, in light of the recent circumstances surrounding Pastor Walker's disappearance, that we put this off until next year. I can't imagine anyone at One Way being in a festive mood."

Lulabelle almost choked on her finger sandwich. She cleared her throat, took a sip of sparkling water, then said, "Mother Kellie, I have already made arrangements for securing the festival location, sponsors, caterer, and the entertainment."

"What?" Mother Kellie replied. "Lulabelle, now how could you have already made arrangements when we have not had the opportunity to meet and vote on this?"

"I told you she already had this church festival planned and paid for," said Melody as she touched up her lip gloss.

Luther just shook his head. "Well," he said, "what was the purpose of this meeting if you already organized everything?"

"Hmph!" Lulabelle huffed. Then she started grabbing coffee cups and snatching plates out of their hands. "Get your sorry behinds out of my house—now!"

Mother Kellie, Melody, and Miss Lillian grabbed their shoes, and Miss Lillian whispered, "I told you the people who live here are wicked."

As they all headed to the foyer, they could see Deacon Evans standing with the front door open, gesturing for them to get out. As they assembled in the driveway, Mother Kellie told them, "It's going to take a boatload of praying folk to get Lulabelle and Deacon Evans to change from their mean-spirited ways—I mean a boatload of folks."

They all laughed as they headed for their vehicles.

THOSE NOSEY MOTHERS

The mothers circled the dark alley for the third time while packed in Mother Kellie's navy-blue minivan. Finally they decided the time was right to get a look inside Pastor Walker's old home. Mother Kellie parked behind the brick ranch house. Before getting out, the mothers joined hands and prayed, asking God not only to protect them but also to forgive them for what they were about to do.

One by one the mothers descended from the van, all dressed in black—and wearing green surgical gloves. Mother Kellie led the way as she opened the gate to enter the backyard. As the mothers tiptoed through the backyard, they heard a loud slam. They froze in their tracks. There was no movement and not a word mumbled—until Mother Millie began to cry and shake.

"I want to go home," she said. "Please take me home! I have never been to jail, and I wouldn't last a night. I have heard the awful stories about old women in jail. Please! Please, Jesus! Hear my cry! Take me home!"

The mothers shushed her and motioned for her to shut up. Then Mother Janie tapped Mother Millie on the shoulder, and when Mother Millie turned around, Mother Janie slapped her. Crying out, Mother Millie almost lost her balance, but Mother Janie grabbed her by both of her arms.

"Millie!" Mother Janie half-whispered, half-growled. "Get yourself together. Woman up, cousin!"

Mother Millie looked Mother Janie in the eyes. "Oh, Janie, I don't know what happened. I just lost it. I promise I won't let you down."

Nodding, Mother Janie said, "Millie, I don't want to have to come back here again, okay?"

"Okay, cousin, okay," Millie said.

Mother Addie then whispered to Mother Kellie that if any other woman would have slapped Mother Millie, Mother Millie would have detached the arm from her body, but she and Mother Janie shared a special bond as first cousins.

Mother Kellie whispered in reply, "Say no more."

Then Mother Addie moved closer to the back door and began picking the lock as Mother Kellie shined a flashlight over the lock. It took Mother Addie less than two minutes to get the lock open. After she turned the doorknob, she gave Mother Kellie a thumbs-up to alert the mothers to get ready to move in and secure it.

As Mother Addie applied pressure on the door to push it open, she gave a grunt. The door wouldn't budge.

Seeing Mother Addie's struggle, Mother Janie moved up front to help.

Mother Addie nodded at her and whispered, "Mother Janie, on the count of three, we push this door open, okay?"

Mother Janie nodded in reply.

"One ... two ... three!" Mother Addie said.

A second later Mothers Addie and Janie found themselves sprawled on the kitchen floor. A light popped on above them.

"Oh, Lord, help us!" Mother Addie cried out.

Gazing up, they saw a strange-looking woman staring them down. The woman standing over them had pink rollers in her hair, wore a pink quilted robe, and sported white bunny slippers. She also held a wooden bat in one hand and her cell phone in the other. As soon as Mother Janie located her glasses next to her on the floor, she realized the woman standing over them was Ms. Roxie, the neighbor from next door.

At the same time, the other mothers had poured in to help Mothers Addie and Janie up.

"Good gracious, woman!" Mother Janie said to Ms. Roxie. "You could've given me a heart attack! Why didn't you say something standing there like that?"

"Give you a heart attack? What about me!" Ms. Roxie said. "I have permission to be in here and you don't. I could've called the police right now!"

Mother Janie rolled her eyes and frowned at her. "Could've, would've, should've! Don't start with me."

Bat and cell phone still in hand, Ms. Roxie crossed her arms over her chest and glared at Mother Janie.

Mother Kellie stepped forward. "Ms. Roxie, thank you for not calling the police. We are the Mothers' Board from One Way. You know ... the church where Pastor Walker pastors—or pastored."

"Mm-hm, yeah, I know the church, and I know who you all are. You all keep running pastor after pastor away. It's a shame how you all treat the pastors up there and then pretend to be the saints of the church." Ms. Roxie paused and shook her head. "Now I see why you all can't keep a pastor. With snooping members—breaking-and-entering members!—who in their right mind would want to stay pastor and be treated like a criminal?"

Mother Kellie gave a clipped sigh and tried again: "Ms. Roxie, we are here out of concern for our pastor. Yes, you are right. Our church has seen many pastors, and we the mothers are not proud about it. We sat idle and kept quiet. Now we are reclaiming our church, and we need to be certain that Pastor Walker was not a victim of any shady business or wrongdoing by any One Way member. We, the mothers, are finally taking a stand to get to the bottom of this mess, even if it means snooping. We are not happy about this, but we figured there have to be some clues in this house to tell us what really happened to Pastor Walker. "

As Ms. Roxie processed what Mother Kellie had just said, she looked at each of the mothers standing before her. Finally she slammed her baseball bat onto the kitchen counter and shouted, "Child, why didn't you say that early on? I thought you mothers were criminals too. Thank God somebody at that church got some sense. I want to help, because God knows …" Ms. Roxie stopped and began sobbing. "God knows that Pastor Walker kept my grass cut, raked my leaves, and shoveled my snow. He always checked on me to make sure I was okay. His momma always made sure I had Sunday dinner. Those Walkers were good to me. I haven't seen Ms. Walker since this happened. I know she got to be aching something fierce about her son. Well, Mothers, do what you came to do, and I am going to get out of your way. If you need me, just stop by and knock."

"Oh, thank you so much, and our hearts and prayers are with you, Ms. Roxie," Mother Kellie said. "And before you leave, Ms. Roxie … Did you notice anything odd about Pastor Walker before he disappeared? Maybe visitors to his home in the last couple of weeks? Any detail, no matter how small, may be of importance."

She shook her head. "Nothing!" She swung her head around and put the baseball bat on her shoulder as she began to leave, but then she halted and turned back around. "Hold on now! There was a woman here a couple of weeks ago. Didn't think anything of it at the time, but maybe it will help you all. It was a Saturday night—I remember because I was waiting for *Saturday Night Live* to come on. Well, she arrived before the eleven o'clock news on Channel 9. What struck me as odd was that she had a key." Ms. Roxie nodded, then said, "She went in the front door and stayed until the news went off. I stepped out to have a cigarette and a beer before *Saturday Night Live* came on, and I saw her leaving. She was walking toward her white Cadillac, and I asked her what she was doing in Pastor Walker's home. She claimed she was conducting a 'wellness check.' I looked at her and said, 'Right … jump-off, tryst, affair, booty call, and now the middle-aged social elite have labeled it as a midnight wellness check.' I mean, I—"

Mother Kellie cut in and said, "This makes absolutely no sense."

The other mothers all talked and murmured among themselves, but then Mother Kellie encouraged Ms. Roxie to continue.

"Well, the woman was visibly peeved at me for making that statement. She walked over to my fence and handed me her business card and told me she was at Pastor Walker's home on official business. I read her card and looked up at her and said, 'Ms. Evans, you are a grown woman. You don't owe me no explanation as to why you are creeping out of Pastor Walker's home in the middle of the night.' I grabbed my beer and went back inside my home."

"Oh my word!" Mother Kellie said. "Evans!" She turned and looked at the other mothers. "Got to be Lulabelle! Heavens, I can't believe this!"

All the other mothers started jabbering, but then Ms. Roxie spoke over them.

"Yep, that's right—her card said *Lulabelle Evans*. Also, Mothers, I don't know if this helpful or not, but a couple of months ago, Pastor Walker came out of his home early one morning with a younger woman and walked her to a car parked on the street out front. He said good-bye and told her she deserved better and to do better. I think he called her 'Lena.' I got a good look at her. She had a busted lip and a black eye. To this day I don't know if she had it before she arrived or if it happened in Pastor Walker's home."

The mothers erupted with a mix of gasps, cries, murmurs, and whispers.

Mother Kellie finally quieted them all down, then turned and asked Ms. Roxie in half-hushed tone, "Are you sure her name was Lena?"

Ms. Roxie nodded. "Yes, I'm positive, because I love me some Lena Horne, God rest her soul. I remember thinking the only other person I know by that name is the famous Lena Horne."

Silence filled the room. All the mothers knew it seemed too much a coincidence for this "Lena" not to be Lena Dobson, a faithful member of One Way—and for many years the girlfriend of an abusive man.

"Well, Mothers, that's all I got," Ms. Roxie said. "Good luck to you." And with that she departed out the back door.

The mothers stood there, looking at each other in disbelief, but then Mother Kellie said, "Let's get moving, Mothers!"

The mothers hurried into action. They hung black trash bags over the windows so that they could begin their search for clues. After the bags were taped over each window, the mothers turned on all the lights and began their investigation.

"My God, Mothers, this place looks empty," Mother Janie said. "I don't see no furniture—nothing but trash!"

"We still need to search this place from top to bottom," said Mother Kellie.

The mothers broke into groups as they moved from room to room, searching through trash, closets, drawers, and cabinets. Mother Janie and Mother Millie started in the kitchen, and right away, Mother Millie discovered a pink glass mug with the initial "L" on it, sitting on the counter. The mug had wine-colored lipstick on it, which would naturally indicate the pink mug belonged to or was used by a woman. Mother Millie and Mother Janie looked at each other and shouted for Mother Kellie.

A moment later Mother Kellie scurried into the kitchen and spotted the mug.

Mother Millie pointed at it and asked, "Could this prove that Lulabelle was here?"

Mother Kellie's eyebrows arched, and she said, "Mother Millie, get a picture of this mug from different angles quick and then bag this evidence up—and please make sure you keep your gloves on the whole time."

While Mother Millie preserved the first piece of evidence, Mother Janie continued searching the kitchen.

"Good job, ladies!" Mother Kellie said. "Keep at it."

Then she left the kitchen and headed down the short hall to a half-bath. Nothing of any interest called to her there, so she returned to the living room, where she pulled out her cell phone and called

Mother Mae, who had refused to come because she did not want to be a part of "breaking and entering." Mother Kellie had agreed to let Mother Mae off the hook because they needed someone on the outside in case something unexpected came up. Mother Kellie failed to mention that Mae's knowledge of the event might make her an accomplice anyway—some things were better left unsaid. So the mothers had agreed to call Mother Mae with news of any findings.

"Mother Mae," Mother Kellie said, "we have found some evidence, but we are still searching. I will call you once I get everyone home."

The mothers spent the next thirty minutes searching for more clues. Mother Kellie located an empty diet strawberry soda can in the trash bin. She decided to photograph it and then remove it and place it in her evidence bag. She wasn't sure if it meant anything, but she knew that Pastor Walker was a diabetic and did not drink anything sugary.

As the mothers concluded their search, Mother Kellie stopped next door to Ms. Roxie's place to thank her and retrieve the business card. Unfortunately Ms. Roxie was unable to find the business card but promised to call Mother Kellie right away if she saw anything suspicious.

The mothers dozed on and off as Mother Kellie sped down the alley and onto the freeway to get everyone back home as quickly as possible.

Meanwhile Brother Ben waited at his home for Mother Kellie to return, pacing the driveway he and Mother Kellie shared. In addition to Mother Kellie being his fiancée, she was also his next-door neighbor. Finally he heard the noisy engine of Mother Kellie's old minivan speeding down the dark cul-de-sac. A relieved grin laced his lips as he stood back and watched her zip into the garage, with her giving a quick wave on her way past. Brother Ben raced into the garage before she put the door down and then he opened the driver's door.

"Kellie, I was sure worried about you and the mothers. How did everything go?"

After clicking the remote to put the garage door down, Mother Kellie stepped out, kissed him on the cheek, said "Hey, baby," and then hurried to the back of the van and opened the hatch. After she told Brother Ben about the conversation they'd had with Ms. Roxie, she pulled out two black garbage bags and showed him the evidence.

Without touching anything, he said, "Now, Kellie, that 'L' could stand for Lulabelle, Leon, Lena, Lillian, Lisa, Luther, or who knows. We can't afford to jump to conclusions. We also can't jump to conclusions regarding Lena's and Lulabelle's visit to Pastor Walker's home. We need more conclusive information. Understood?"

Mother Kellie sighed, then said, "Yes, Ben. But you have to admit this is worth looking into, right?"

Brother Ben nodded. "Yeah, you're right. We have to pay closer attention to anyone whose name starts with an 'L' at church."

"Got that right," Mother Kellie said.

Brother Ben held open the door that led into the kitchen. Mother Kellie moved past him, her mind already racing with what she would tell all the mothers at their weekly meeting, to be held at her house the very next morning. With a breakfast meal to plan, she said "Good night" to Brother Ben, gave him a quick kiss, then got busy in the kitchen.

Even with a short night of sleep, Mother Kellie got up early to print off photos of the clues—and to get breakfast started, with a Crock-Pot of grits boiling, eggs in the skillet, and bacon in the oven. She knew the mothers would be tapping at her door any minute. Brother Ben had brought tables and chairs from his condo over to her place to set up for the mothers.

As Mother Kellie was setting the table, she heard a car door slam. She peeked out her dining-room window and saw Deacon King circling the van to unload the mothers. Mother Kellie shouted for Ben to grab the door as she moved the food from the stove to the table.

One by one, the mothers came in. Mother Mae came in first with two pans full of tall, flaky, buttery homemade biscuits, with homemade strawberry preserves. She hollered, "Mother Kellie, you sure got it smelling good up in here."

"Thank you, Mother Mae. Let me grab your jacket."

Then Mother Kellie nudged Brother Ben, who in turn told Deacon King, "Deacon, let's grab our plates and go next door. I got the game on tape."

"That sounds like a winner," Deacon King said. "Now, Mothers, when you are ready, come get me."

Several of the mothers—the ones not absorbed in exchanging recipes and stories of sundry body aches—waved to the two men and told them to have fun.

The mothers took their seats around the table and began passing the food as Mother Kellie updated Mother Mae with the latest info. After Mother Mae processed the information about the clues and the conversation with Ms. Roxie, she blanked out in deep thought.

"Mother Mae! Mother Mae, do you hear what I am saying?" Mother Kellie said.

Mother Mae nodded. "Yes, I heard everything." She looked around the group. "Mothers, we must be careful and private about this conversation and any information that we discover from this point forward. Please carry a pad with you at all times and take notes of anything that sounds questionable. Many of you have camera cell phones, so take pictures. If you don't, we also brought disposable cameras. They're on the table over here, so please take one and keep it in your pocketbook. Please don't steal anything that might be a clue; rather, take a picture of it. Okay?"

Everyone nodded or spoke their agreement.

"Then," Mother Mae said, "Mothers, let's pray so that we can eat this wonderful breakfast."

After they ate, cleared the table, and cleaned the kitchen, the mothers were escorted back to Mother Kellie's solarium. Once they entered it, they saw that Mother Kellie had on display the evidence they had picked up from Pastor Walker's home. Mother Kellie cautioned everyone not to touch anything, but to get a good look at everything.

As everyone took a seat in the sun-filled room that overlooked Mother Kellie's cozy fenced-in backyard, Mother Mae stood before the ladies while Mother Kellie handed out post-card-sized photos of the clues.

Mother Mae began by saying, "Mothers, we must now operate undercover. We must look for any member who has a pink decorative mug and any member drinking diet strawberry soda or the same brand as this soda. You need to inform me, Mother Janie, or Mother Kellie as soon as possible if you see either of these things or anything else that seems suspicious. These are the clues we have before us, and it's imperative that we start taking a second look at the members of the church whose names began with 'L.' We have a list of those members in the packet of photos that Mother Kellie just handed out. Remember, confidentiality is necessary to our finding out what really happened to Pastor Walker. Okay, does anyone have any questions?"

No one said anything, and a few shook their heads.

"Well, then, let's go home," Mother Mae said.

Mother Kellie picked up her cell phone and called Brother Ben. "Ben, please tell Deacon King the meeting is over, and the mothers are ready to head home."

"Okay, we will be outside waiting at the van," replied Brother Ben.

The mothers prayed together and then embraced each other. They departed for home with a clear mission on their minds.

LOOSE LIPS

Mother Millie sat in a plush, black leather chair at Hot Rod's Beauty Salon, getting a touch-up from her favorite stylist, Henry—and bursting with news she couldn't help but share. She began to brag about how the mothers had collected evidence from Reverend Walker's home and that they were on the verge of solving the case. Unbeknownst to Mother Millie, seated next to her was Vickie Gilbert, one of Lulabelle's closest friends from high school.

Hot Rod himself was putting highlights in Vickie's hair, but he was also quite involved in a tense long-distance call with his grandmother, so he remained oblivious to Mother Millie's chatter. She babbled on and on for more than thirty minutes about how the mothers had devised a plan to get into Pastor Walker's home, unaware that Vickie had focused in on her monologue.

Vickie did her best to tune out Hot Rod's ongoing phone call in an attempt to listen to Millie's every word. Though she missed some, she certainly got the gist of the comments. Mother Millie told Henry how the mothers got Pastor Walker's neighbor to talk.

Once Mother Millie was placed under the dryer and unable to hear, Vickie asked Henry, "Boy, you sure got Mother's hair looking good and healthy. Isn't she on the esteemed Mothers' Board at One Way?"

Henry nodded. "Yes. Mother Millie, God bless her heart, is a part of that glorious Mothers' Board at One Way. She has been on it for years. Those mothers had the blues after Pastor Walker mysteriously disappeared. So it's good to see her happy. If anybody is going to find out about Pastor Walker, I believe those mothers will do it. They have the resolve and intellect to bring their pastor back home."

"Henry, I guess all we can do is pray for them. Sounds like they are getting close to finding Pastor Walker. I will keep that church in prayer."

Henry invited his next customer into his chair, pointed his comb toward Vickie, and said, "Yes, honey, prayer solves problems. Do you hear me? I use to drink, smoke, gossip, and lie, but Mother Millie and those virtuous mothers prayed those demons out of me. So when I say prayer solves problem, I know. One Way has a heap of problem members. So we all must stay prayerful to help One Way and those precious mothers."

Vickie nodded and mumbled "Amen" as Henry began working on his next client. Vickie's mind, though, had begun percolating about the juicy gossip she was going to have to share with Lulabelle.

By this time Mother Millie had fallen fast asleep under the dryer, feeling content and happy to have been in the limelight for a few minutes while she related her big news about Pastor Walker. Finally, after about forty-five minutes under the dryer, Henry gently woke her up.

Vickie stuck around a little longer after Hot Rod had finished her hair, and got her nails done, hoping that Mother Millie and Henry would resume their conversation.

Mother Millie didn't disappoint, and she picked up where she had left off: "Henry, the last person in Pastor Walker's home left a lipstick-covered pink mug with the letter 'L' inscribed on it. We gave that mug to Mother Kellie, and her boyfriend is going to have a fingerprint test done on it. Once the results from the test are in, we are going to be much closer to finding out who was involved in Pastor Walker's disappearance. The number one person on my list is that Lulabelle Evans."

"Say no more, Mother Millie. That woman puts corrupt in corruption. You feel me?"

"Henry, I feel you. She has been blocking the church's success for years."

"Mother Millie, it's going to be okay. God don't like ugly, and ugly is written all over Deacon Evans' face. Every church has its drama; it's just unfortunate that One Way is the biggest church around here and that news about One Way spreads like desert wildfires in July."

Henry spun Mother Millie around in his chair, teasing her 1970s feathered hairstyle. He then sprayed her down and turned her to the mirror and said, "Mother Millie, it was a pleasure doing your beautiful hair again. I wish more of my clients would follow your lead and take better care of their hair. You are a joy to have as a client."

Mother Millie laughed. "Oh, now stop it, Henry! You going to make me blush and give you my entire retirement check."

After Mother Millie paid Henry, he gave her a kiss on the cheek and helped her out of the chair. Mother Millie's granddaughter, Vivian, waited in the parking lot for her. She waved to Henry and greeted her grandmother with a hug.

"Granny, Henry sure hooked up your hair."

"I told you that boy could do some hair," said Mother Millie as she tottered down the steps, holding on tight to Vivian.

After Henry watched Vivian and Mother Millie pull out of the salon's parking lot, he went out back, took a smoke break, and got on his cell phone. "Child, I got some hot gossip for you! You not going to believe what one of your church's mothers just told me. Let me tell you what those nosey mothers have been up to. Child, you better stand up for this one, because this is going to rock you up out of your rocker. You hear me?"

Once Henry finished the phone call, he went back inside to work—and proceeded to tell his next five customers about what Mother Millie told him. As the story traveled on from there, it began to get more and more convoluted. The sales clerk at the South Town Beauty Supply Store was overheard telling a customer that the mothers of One Way found a beer mug with the letter "L" on it on Pastor Walker's porch and they believed the beer mug belonged to Lulabelle. Further, a rumor started that the mothers were having a lip analysis done and would know the last lips that were on the mug.

After several attempts to reach Lulabelle, Vickie had no choice but to tell Deacon Evans of the news she'd overheard at Hot Rod's. After Deacon Evans heard the story, he told Vickie that he appreciated the information and would relay it to Lulabelle. Deacon Evans began to wonder if this could have been Lulabelle's pink mug. His mind began racing with crazy thoughts about her somehow being involved. *Would she be willing to do something so callous? I know she didn't like Pastor Walker, but would she be capable of such an act?* He immediately dismissed it, but kept returning to the thought. He decided to tell her and closely observe her reaction. Once he sat Lulabelle down and told her what Vickie heard, she laughed.

"Baby," Lulabelle said, "Vickie has been on anxiety medication for years because she is always hearing voices. I am sure this is one of those episodes. We both know those mothers aren't capable of investigating anything." Lulabelle saw the serious stare on Deacon Evans' face and added, "Harold, I know you aren't thinking that I had something to do with this. Now I have done some questionable things in my past, but I would never do any harm to a man of God, let alone my church. It troubles me that you would even for a moment think I would be capable of such an act."

Deacon Evans thought, *Lu, you have asked me to partake in some pretty shady stuff, and you have the nerve to question why I thought about it!*

"Harold!" Lulabelle shouted.

Deacon Evans jumped in his seat and said, "Sorry, Lu, I was lost in thought there. I know you didn't have anything to do with this. I was just thinking about poor Vickie. I totally forgot about her hearing voices. What a crying shame."

Deacon Evans rose from his seat to go into the kitchen, but Lulabelle still didn't quite feel convinced that he believed she was innocent.

Meanwhile Mother Janie got a call from her beautician, Louise: "Janie, that big-mouth cousin of yours, Millie, has been spilling the beans about you mothers. I told you and Mother Mae she can't hold her water, so how you expect her to hold secrets?"

"Louise, settle down. Don't get yourself worked up over Millie. Now tell me what you got?"

"I just had a chat with Henry—you know, from Hot Rod's—in the lottery line at the One Way Quick Stop. He said Mother Millie told him that the mothers illegally searched Pastor Walker's home and uncovered evidence—specifically a mug with the name 'Lulabelle' on it, and the police will be getting back with you about whose fingers were the last to touch it. Now you know if Henry told me, he has already told ten others."

"Hot dang! Just wait until I get a hold of her," said Mother Janie. "Now, Louise, please, if you truly love the Lord and One Way, don't let this information go any further."

"Mother Janie, I love you, Mother Mae, the Lord, and all of One Way; you have my word on my second and third ex-husbands' graves that I will not tell a soul."

Mother Janie began pacing her dining room floor with her cordless phone stuck to her ear, still reeling from the news. "Louise, I got to get off this phone and call Millie. I will see you next Tuesday morning for a wash and curl."

"Okay. Good-bye, Janie."

Mother Janie kept pacing and just could not stop herself from feeling that sick feeling of agitation and worry. So she decided to go make herself a cup of coffee before she called Millie. She needed a moment to collect her thoughts and to calm down so that she didn't blast Millie too strongly when she finally called her.

After her cup of coffee and some quiet time, Mother Janie picked up the phone and used speed-dial for Mother Millie.

"Millie, this is Janie. How you doing, sweetie?"

"I'm doing okay for an old lady. What's on your mind, Janie?"

"Millie, I just heard from a reliable source that you were down at Hot Rod's running off at the mouth about what the mothers specifically told you not to discuss with anyone. Don't you dare try to lie your way out of this, Millie, because they told me all the facts that we discussed at Mother Kellie's home, and nobody but you on the Mothers' Board patronizes that drug-front beauty salon. Now tell me I'm wrong!"

Sniffling into the phone, Millie said, "Janie, every time I go down to that salon, I feel pressured to tell Henry what's going on at One Way. Lately I didn't have anything good or juicy to report, so I told him about our adventure. I'm so sorry. I just feel awful." Then she began crying.

Mother Janie shook her head and nearly shouted, "Millie, those tears don't mean anything to me! I'mma tell you like this: we the mothers can't afford to have loose lips on board our ship, cause loose lips are known to sink ships. So this is your only warning. If any more news gets back to me or any of the mothers, we will have to pull your Mothers' Board membership card. Do you understand?"

Millie sniffled a few times, then responded, "I do and I promise not to let you down. I am so sorry. And … Janie?"

"Yes, Millie?"

"Who told you that Hot Rod's was a drug-front beauty salon?"

"None of your business. You keep going down there in that bad neighborhood getting your hair done, you going to be caught up in a drug deal gone bad. But don't try to change the subject. When the urge to lie or be boastful come on, recite this phrase: 'The Lord is my shepherd; I shall not want to lie or be boastful.' Millie, this will help you to deal with that demon that is lying dormant on your tongue. Cousin, you have to fight it. Now look, I got to go, but please don't make me have to pull your Mothers' Board membership card, because it won't be pretty, okay? Now good night, Millie."

"Hold on, Janie! Can we talk for a little while longer?"

"Millie, I have been waiting all day to watch *Dr. Phil*. If you need to talk some more, talk to Jesus. He is always ready to listen. Tell him all of your problems, because I can't handle all of the drama going in and out of your life right now. Okay?"

"Yes, Janie, thank you."

As Mother Janie went into her living room to turn the channel to *Dr. Phil*, she felt all stirred up inside just thinking about Mother Millie. "Millie is a mess. Knowing Millie, she probably on the phone with Henry right now telling him what we just talked about. Lord, bless my cousin."

DRAMA IN THE PULPIT

For the past two Sundays the pulpit had sat there dark and empty during service—with the few members present singing together and then Deacon Evans giving announcements before one of the mothers prayed to bring the service to a close. So on this unseasonably cool and windy Sunday morning, it felt a little strange to know that some outsider would be invading One Way to stand behind the sacred pulpit. Word had traveled quickly through the church family over the week that Lulabelle's cousin would be preaching at One Way on Sunday, and that she might even try to sneak him in as pastor.

Mother Karen said her daughter's baby daddy had reported on Lulabelle's preaching cousin: "That man may be a sharp dresser, a professor of words, and good looking, but he is an awful singer and preacher," said the baby daddy.

Lulabelle made her grand entrance into the church, modeling her floor-length white fur coat with matching hat as she strolled down the center aisle carrying her fire-engine-red snakeskin briefcase, ignoring the seated members.

Last winter Lulabelle and Deacon Evans' matching sable fur coats went missing after they checked them in with the ushers. Lulabelle swore the ushers threw their coats away, but the ushers said it was an honest mistake that could easily happen because they checked more than three hundred coats each week. Of course, Lulabelle had the church reimburse her and Deacon Evans for the cost of their coats. And to ensure this never occurred again, Lulabelle made a point to wear her coat during service. Deacon Evans opted to keep his coat in his car.

Then there was Lulabelle's briefcase: it accompanied her to the ladies room, the dining hall, and all church functions and meetings. The few members—strategically seated in view of her opening and closing it—reported that she stored her Bible, makeup, breath mints, financial books, and bank deposit slips in it. But to hear Lulabelle tell it, one would think she had millions of dollars stashed there.

Lena Dobson, the faithful member who had been in an abusive relationship for years, rushed up to Lulabelle before she sat down. "Sister Evans, I heard you were now going to be spearheading the domestic violence project that Pastor Walker started. Is that true?

"Yes, dear," answered Lulabelle, looking down at Lena.

"Oh, thank you! And I … I wondered if maybe I could talk to you. I am having a hard time at home. I just need someone to talk to, and I thought maybe I could talk to you since you are now over the project."

Lulabelle drew back and eyed Lena. "Child, please. Do I look like a social worker?

Lena nodded. "I know you're not a social worker, but I really need some advice."

Now Lulabelle gave a loud sigh. "Lena, the entire church knows that you live with a man that beats you. Frankly, I find this story ridiculous. Pastor Walker might have fallen for your song and dance, but I'm not. Here is my advice: leave him! Now, excuse me, I am looking for my cousin."

Lulabelle turned to the rear of the church. Lena stood there for a moment, shocked, then finally returned to her seat, heartbroken that Lulabelle couldn't find it in her saved soul to listen to a church member in need.

Soon enough Lulabelle's preaching cousin, Edwin Davis, drove up to the church in a late-model white Lexus. He and his wife got out of the car and marched into the sanctuary, and some of the members in the vestibule gasped. With their noses in the air and eyes focused on the dark pulpit, Reverend Davis and his wife, both in matching tan fur coats and tan suits, marched right down the center aisle. Reverend Davis' wife was rolling a conspicuous white suitcase. They, of course, were too important to wait on the ushers to direct them to their seats.

His eyes covered by dark glasses, Reverend Davis proceeded down the center aisle of the church, then he coughed to get Lulabelle's attention. Lulabelle stood up and waved them up to her pew. The congregation gave unimpressed stares and frowns as Lulabelle and Deacon Evans showered Reverend and Sister Davis with hugs and kisses.

After Reverend Davis stood in the middle aisle to make sure everyone got a glimpse of him, he removed his fur coat and spun it around as he laid it on the pew in front of him.

Across the aisle from Reverend Davis, Mother Janie snorted a laugh. Then, in a voice loud enough for everyone to hear, she said, "Was that really necessary?"

Reverend Davis looked up as if he were ready to make a move over to the mothers' pew to see who had made such a comment, but he did nothing. As Reverend Davis was about to take his seat, his wife opened the white suitcase to remove his gold cape, which she draped over him. She also removed his 18-karat-gold water pitcher and a glass, along with a bottle of water, which she used to fill the pitcher. As Reverend Davis headed to the pulpit, the pulpit usher, Usher Gibson, stopped him short of the steps.

One Way members knew not to cross Usher Gibson when she told them to shut up, sit down, or move it. Usher Gibson stretched out her white-gloved hand to the shoulder of Reverend Davis and directed him back to his seat. She explained to him in a nice, but stern, tone, "When we are ready for you to occupy the pulpit, we will come for you. For now, the pulpit is to remain vacant until such time. Understood?"

Reverend Davis gave Usher Gibson a "You don't know me" look and said, "Whatever," and then he went back to take a seat next to his wife.

Laughs erupted throughout the congregation.

As Reverend Davis took his seat, Lulabelle made her way up to Usher Gibson and told her, "Don't you ever disrespect my family like that."

Usher Gibson responded, "Careful. I'm not Deacon Evans. I will remove you from the premises if you don't get out of my face."

Lulabelle's breath caught and she mumbled "Well, I never!" with her hands on her hips. She looked up to a stone-faced Usher Gibson, who towered over her, and quickly backed down. Lulabelle caught herself and realized that all eyes were on her and Usher Gibson, so she was careful to give the appearance when she turned around that she had put Usher Gibson in her place, but the congregation knew better.

Lulabelle took her seat and told her cousin, "This is why we need more affluent folk like us up in here, because these members don't know how to talk or act. They must be put in their place."

Reverend Davis looked at Lulabelle and said, "Lu, these dummies are crazy and rude. If I get this pulpit, there will be major changes up in here, you hear me. My first order of business will be those meddling and out-of-control mothers over there."

Lulabelle hollered, "Hallelujah! For once someone is speaking my language up in this church."

The packed sanctuary was warm and bright despite the cold and rain outside. The choir box was full, with 172 members singing praises to the Lord. They sounded even better than usual. For the first time in a while, one could actually feel the Spirit in their singing of "I Will Trust in the Lord." The deacons, though, sped through devotions, because many of them wanted to be home in time to see the baseball game.

As Miss Lillian was reading the church announcements, Lulabelle traipsed down the aisle and handed a note to her.

Miss Lillian accepted the note and asked, "What is it?"

Lulabelle replied, "Just read it."

"First, tell me what it is."

"Miss Lillian, don't play with me. Do your job and read this."

Miss Lillian finished the announcements, then paused and said, "Oops, Sister Lulabelle asked me to read this note, members: 'Our very own smart, loving, and devoted Deacon Evans was selected from a pool of over two hundred deacons to be honored at Ohio's Top Deacons Banquet. Attendance is by invitation only or by purchasing a seat for $100 or a table for $1,000. Please be advised that no church funds will be utilized for this event."

The announcement was met with silence. And with that Miss Lillian took her seat.

It was finally time for Reverend Davis to take the pulpit, but before he did, Lulabelle made a point to formally introduce her cousin to the church. After she strolled down the center aisle, she grabbed the microphone and proceeded to the podium.

Resting her index cards on the podium, she began to recite the following: "Good morning, One Way, and all of our many friends. This morning I bring to you my second cousin, Edwin Davis. Edwin is a graduate of Middleton State University in sociology. Edwin also holds a graduate degree in divinity from Chicago Holy University. Edwin is a gifted singer who has been singing all of his life. Edwin has been preaching now for three years, and he and his wife are looking for a new church home. Edwin loves the Lord like we all do and would make a great candidate for pastor here at One Way. Please join me with an applause as we welcome my family, my cousin, Reverend Edwin Davis, to the pulpit of One Way. Let all the saints in the sanctuary say 'Welcome, Reverend Davis.'"

The members responded in unison, but with only lukewarm enthusiasm: "Welcome, Reverend Davis."

But Reverend Davis jumped up and shouted, "We about to have service up in here!"

Usher Gibson escorted him to the pulpit. Evangelist Hattie, seated on the opposite side of the pulpit in front of the choir stand, greeted

Reverend Davis and returned to her seat. Reverend Davis, with a wide grin on his face, adjusted the pulpit microphone and then asked the musicians if they could help him out with a verse of "At the Cross"—because Lulabelle had told him the night before that this was the Mothers' Board's favorite hymn.

Deacon Evans shouted, "Take your time, and sing your song, cousin."

Reverend Davis looked at the musicians and told them, "Excuse me, that is not my key. Please let me lead you."

Melody Note, One Way's minister of music and a classically trained pianist, bit her tongue, literally, to keep herself from saying anything about Reverend Davis' condescending attitude. She just sighed and decided to let him go without music, so she instructed the musicians to take their seats in the congregation, then she did the same.

Reverend Davis went with it and belted out the first few words of the song. The congregation, though, remained quiet—except for Deacon Evans and his wife, although they both stayed seated. Melody shook her head, rolled her eyes, and pulled out her nail file to work on her nails.

Halting the song, Reverend Davis cleared his throat and said, "Members, don't get quiet on me. Let me sing this verse one more time."

It became clear that this man could not sing. Lulabelle had been hoodwinking the members of One Way with her talk of him being a "gifted singer."

Reverend Davis kept swinging his long hair from side to side, hitting unknown notes—and looking like an idiot from some rap video as he removed his jacket and threw it to the floor. He then began unbuttoning his shirt.

The congregation gasped, groaned, looked away, and murmured among themselves.

Then Reverend Davis began shouting, "Let me say it one more time. Let me say it just one more time!"

"Please, Jesus, no more!" shouted Mother Millie.

The other mothers nodded. However, the rest of the congregation couldn't hear Mother Millie because Reverend Davis was now practically screaming. Finally Lulabelle stood up and swayed to his off-key rendition of "At the Cross," but no one, not even Lulabelle, could save him at this point. The singers and musicians just smirked. Mother Addie turned her hearing aid down. The other mothers looked on in disbelief.

"This is shameful. I hope his sermon is better than his singing," whispered Mother Janie.

"Amen!" responded Mother Mae.

Reverend Davis finally realized his solo was sinking, so he decided to jump into his sermon. His wife signaled for Usher Gibson to take Reverend Davis' gold pitcher and glass. Usher Gibson obliged. After sipping some water and putting his jacket back on, Reverend Davis directed the congregation to Psalm 100. He stumbled over the first five verses, blaming the poor lighting in the pulpit.

"If he would take off those dark glasses, maybe he could see the words he keeps missing," Mother Janie whispered to Mother Mae.

"Hush up, Janie," Mother Mae said, but still laughed.

All of a sudden, there was dead quiet in the sanctuary. Reverend Davis' lips were moving, but no one could hear him. He then spoke a little louder and then as faint as a whisper. This went on for the next twenty minutes. Then when he went back to speaking in a whisper tone, a loud roaring noise erupted from the congregation. To some members the noise seemed similar to agitated horses. The noise became louder and louder, overshadowing Reverend Davis.

As the deacons turned around to investigate what Reverend Davis had already noticed from the pulpit, they found the mothers fast asleep and snoring. Their snores were somehow in sync. Up on stage Evangelist Hattie had also fallen asleep.

Lulabelle huffed and muttered something under her breath, then snapped her fingers for Usher Gibson to do something. Usher Gibson saw Lulabelle, but she turned away and ignored her pleas.

Lulabelle bolted up out her seat, took her hymnal book, and stomped over to the mothers' pew. She slammed the hymnal twice with both hands on the pew in front of them, and whispered, "Wake it up!"

She slammed the hymnal so hard that it startled Mother Addie, who was sitting directly in front of where Lulabelle stood. When Mother Addie awoke and jumped in her seat, she inadvertently slap Lulabelle's hat off her head. The congregation erupted with laughter because Lulabelle's stocking cap had been revealed. She moved quickly to retrieve her hat and take her seat.

Now, out of nowhere, the Spirit moved Reverend Davis to speak in tongues. As some of the congregation motioned for the ushers to wake up Evangelist Hattie so she could interpret the tongues, Reverend Davis continued. Evangelist Hattie's interpretation skills had always been in question and, once she finally woke up, today proved no different. Evangelist Hattie pulled her personal 18-karat-gold handheld microphone from the white leather "I Love Jesus" oversized tote bag seated on her lap and quickly moved up front to begin interpreting Reverend Davis' sermon. She did a quick "Testing one, two, three" as she tapped her microphone to make sure it was in sync with the church's intercom system. The congregation nodded its approval. Evangelist Hattie looked up to the ceiling. The congregation became quiet. They were waiting to hear a word from the Lord.

As Reverend Davis spoke in tongues again, the congregation shifted their attention to Evangelist Hattie for the meaning. Meanwhile Reverend Davis looked for help from Lulabelle, as he didn't seem to be sure about what was happening. Lulabelle shrugged her shoulders and motioned for him to continue.

Evangelist Hattie raised both of her hands to the sky and said, "Lord, I need a new pair of new shoes."

Silenced again filled the sanctuary. The mothers' began looking at one another, unsure if they had correctly heard Evangelist Hattie. Reverend Davis gave Evangelist Hattie a puzzled look and continued.

Evangelist Hattie paused and looked down toward the ground and shouted, "Someone in here is in need of a blessing! Saints, I repeat, someone in here is in need of a blessing. Please stand if this is you."

Everyone in the congregation stood. Reverend Davis looked overjoyed by the congregation's response. He again took his jacket off and threw it to the floor, then continued.

Evangelist Hattie shouted as she pointed in the direction of the choir box, "You, standing over here, are weed-heads, chronic lovers, crack addicts, alcoholics, free-basers, gamblers, adulterers, and two- and three-time losers."

With plenty of muttering and grumbling, the congregation and the mothers fell back into their seats in disbelief of the words that Evangelist Hattie was spewing. As the choir members took their seats, Reverend Davis screamed, "FATHER, HELP THIS CHURCH!"

Evangelist Hattie shouted, "Don't hide now. Stand up! Face your demons. God knows all. He knows where you were last night, Sister Mabel. Brother Marvin, don't tip out now. The Father knows what you did last weekend at the Holiday Inn on Dayton Road, and he knows what's at home underneath your mattress, Brother Sam."

The embarrassed choir members stood in shock.

Reverend Davis hurried and grabbed his holy oil, then had the choir members come out of the choir box and form a single-file line to be anointed with oil. After each choir member was anointed, Reverend Davis had each stand before the congregation as he prayed over them in tongues.

Evangelist Hattie interpreted his prayer as follows: "Lord, help our choir members. One by one, they need you. They stand before you Sunday after Sunday not in tune with your Word—not even in tune with the music. Although they physically stand before you each Sunday, they are not here spiritually. Bring them back in. Please, Lord, bring them back in. Bring Sister Mabel back in. She knows she had no business being where she was until 2:00 a.m. this morning. Help her, Lord. Brother Marvin spent the last two weekends doing some ungodly things with some ungodly women. Reel him back in, Father. That stuff that Brother Sam has hiding under his mattress, Lord, burn it. Lord, it has clouded his judgment so that he can't remember the simple verses to his solo. Lord, help this tone-deaf choir. The musicians can only do so much. Help them Lord to find you, and then—and only then—will they be able to sing your praises. Choir, let the tears flow. Choir members, let the tears flow. Choir members, release the jealousy, hate, envious attitudes, and the shadiness, and accept Christ. Amen."

Evangelist Hattie then shook Reverend Davis' hand.

"Sister, you are amazing. You and I work well together," Reverend Davis said.

She shook her head. "I work for the Lord. I don't work for man. Plus, I couldn't get a reading on any of the foolishness you were churning out up there. Reverend Davis, you need to stop playing with the Lord and have a seat."

His eyes wide and his mouth hanging open, Reverend Davis went back to his seat, even as the embarrassed choir did the same.

After everyone had been seated, Reverend Davis rose and returned to the podium to offer his final comments and benediction. He took off his glasses, tapped the podium with his index finger, and released a sigh as he scanned the congregation. "I am very concerned about the lack of church etiquette I witnessed here today. Church, you will continue to run off good preachers if you don't know how to behave." Then he pointed to the Mothers' Board. "If you mothers could wake up and stay up during service, maybe you could resolve these issues that are weighing down One Way."

The mothers looked at each other.

"Nah, he, a visiting minister, couldn't have been talking about us in our very own church," said Mother Janie.

Mother Mae nodded. "I don't think he will be coming back."

Reverend Davis went on. "Take it from someone who knows church etiquette. One Way needs to pay close attention to Harold and Lulabelle Evans. They exhibit fine church etiquette, and One Way could learn a lot by observing them."

The members of the congregation could only shake their heads and roll their eyes.

As the reverend lifted his hands to give the benediction, he looked out at the annoyed crowd and shouted, "Good day!"

He departed the pulpit, and Deacon Evans rushed to him with his coat and briefcase. "Boy, we ain't had good preaching and singing like that in years."

Lulabelle concurred with an "Amen!"

Deacon Evans and Lulabelle then pushed Reverend Davis and his wife out the side door to avoid any confrontation with the members.

Mother Kellie looked at Brother Ben and said, "Did I hear Deacon and Sister Evans right? That man came in here with a bad spirit. He looked down on our church the moment he walked through the sanctuary door, and the Lord showed us exactly who and what he was."

Brother Ben said, "I felt the same way. I felt personally attacked by his classless actions."

"Come on, baby. Time for dinner at Mother Janie's," said Mother Kellie as she took Brother Ben's hand.

Mother Kellie and Brother Ben were considered to be the sweetest couple at One Way. Brother Ben was frequently observed opening her car door, opening any other door she was about to enter, patiently holding her purse, and tending to whatever the need was.

Brother Ben and Mother Kellie got in their car and sped down One Way Lane, heading to Mother Janie's house for dinner. During the car ride they joked about how awful Lulabelle's cousin had sung their favorite hymn.

Every other Sunday after church, Mother Janie hosted dinner at her home for the mothers and Brother Ben. At the table today the aroma of Mother Janie's fried chicken serenaded everyone.

After prayer Mother Mae immediately jumped in and asked, "What was Reverend Davis trying to accomplish this morning? That is not the kind of pastor we need at One Way."

"I think the Evanses are testing the waters to see if we are on our toes. They are very eager to name One Way's next pastor," said Mother Kellie.

Brother Ben nodded. "True, though I doubt today's incident with Reverend Davis was meant to do any harm. More likely they were merely reminding us they still got a dog in this fight."

For the next five minutes all they heard was silverware tapping plates.

Finally Brother Ben broke the silence. "Mothers, I just don't understand how One Way got to this point. Please, somebody, fill in the blanks for me?"

Mother Janie filled his glass with freshly squeezed lemonade and said, "Mother Mae, break it down for Brother Ben."

Mother Mae gave a short nod, then took a deep breath. "One Way Church of the Lord has endured ten solid years of mismanagement, reorganization, pastors abruptly quitting with no notice, and the deacons treating these issues as personal and confidential matters that are of no concern to the congregation. After sitting quietly for ten years of this drama, we, the Mothers' Board, have been forced to regroup and redefine our role to get One Way on the right track. We plan to get to the root of this matter and restore One Way to its place in God's will."

"Amen," replied many of the mothers, while others said, "That's right!"

Brother Ben jumped in and said, "Mother Mae, I now understand."

Mother Janie said, "I guess we got a little lazy, tired, and comfortable in this rut."

Mother Kellie said, "We got a lot of people at One Way thinking they are in charge of things. There is no Christ in their behavior. When I reflect on some of the ongoing problems, it is hard to understand how we sat idle and watched our church membership decrease from an all-time high of 850 active members weekly, to barely 150 members some weeks. You can't go by today's high attendance, since most everyone came out to see that circus!"

"Mm-hmm," Mother Mae said.

"For instance," Mother Kellie went on, "our mass choir, under the strict leadership of Melody Note for the last fifteen years, has suffered an unfortunate loss of choir members due to Melody's harsh criticism and her ear for perfection. Melody has been a mixed blessing to the church. She is a trained musician and can brighten the mood of the congregation with her gift for picking 'lift me up' songs. On the other hand she has been toxic to the choir's success. Melody is a hot mess. Melody has married more One Way men than I care to count. She very seldom smiles, and she is known to break choir members down to tears with her unruly and critical comments. But she is a gifted singer and musician. In addition to playing the piano, she also plays the guitar, violin, and saxophone. She regards the mass choir as her personal choir. If a church engagement does not fit into her schedule, the choir will not be in attendance at the church function. All church engagements that require the choir must be coordinated and approved by Melody.

"I remember when members could join the choir even if they couldn't sing. Now, for church members who want to sing for the glory of God, if they can't carry a tune, they will not be singing in One Way's choir. Melody offers no positive feedback or constructive criticism; she is cut and dry with members wishing to try out for the choir. Melody once stopped the choir in mid-song during the church's anniversary and told them they were off tune and not paying attention to her cues, so she dismissed them from the choir box. Then she packed up her briefcase and purse and left the sanctuary for home." Mother Kellie sighed and shook her head.

"What a shame," Brother Ben said.

A full and relaxed Mother Janie now joined in the discussion: "Mothers, let's take a look at our usher board. The usher board, under the leadership of Vanessa Gibson, has maintained the same ten members for over twenty years. Our ushers are known for bullying and shoving folks. They seat you where you don't want to be seated and move you just when you get comfortable. When you signal for an usher, they outright ignore you. When you don't need an usher, they appear out of nowhere, demanding you to wake up, shut up, or they confiscate your cell phone, chewing gum, mints, or candy. How can we expect people to come back if we don't make them feel welcome and special from the minute they step through the door? Mothers, we got work to do."

The mothers all chimed in their agreement.

Mother Janie continued. "The church trustees handle the church finances under the direction of Sister Lulabelle Evans, Deacon Evans' perfect and saintly wife. Everyone at One Way knows that Lulabelle runs the church through her husband's position as chairman of the Deacons' Board and her position of chairwoman of the Trustee Board. The power and influence she has over her husband and the Trustee Board leads her to believe she is the most powerful woman at One Way. Our trustees are known for some mean-spirited tactics when it comes to managing the church's finances. Should you present a bounced check to the church, Lulabelle will have your name, church photo, and a copy of your check enlarged and placed inside the church's weekly bulletin until the check has been paid. Lulabelle has the deacons use yellow markers to detect counterfeit bills when members place cash in the offering buckets. How embarrassing is that when our visitors see them holding money up to the ceiling, checking for counterfeits. The control that Lulabelle exhibits over the church's finances has forced many of our friends and family to leave One Way. Many members often question the internal controls over the church's finances, but never get an appropriate or direct response.

"Lulabelle's ruthless acts included her canceling our youth summer retreat to Orlando, Florida. After One Way's youth successfully raised more than $13,000 by hosting services, carrying out fundraisers, and obtaining donations, they were told that the church trustees implemented a moratorium on all spending until further notice because the tithes and offerings from the previous month did not meet the trustees' monthly projections. No further discussions were permitted.

"Mothers, it is our duty to steer our beloved church back onto the road of glory. Mothers, we must pray and speak to One Way's deliverance." Mother Janie looked around the room at her supporters.

All the mothers shouted "Amen!" or "Glory!" or "Praise him!" or "Preach it, Janie!"

Encouraged, Mother Janie continued. "Mothers, the congregation will have to rely on us to get the truth, because those deacons can't be trusted. We must ask God to show us the way through this ordeal so that we cause no more harm and embarrassment to One Way. Right now, One Way is temporarily stained, but I know a God that removes stains. What you say, Mothers?"

More shouts filled the room. Mother Janie went into the kitchen and quickly returned with a tray of sweet potato pie and pound cake.

DOMESTIC VIOLENCE PROJECT

The local domestic violence shelter had previously asked Pastor Walker and One Way to host its first annual Southside Community Domestic Violence Workshop, in hopes of addressing domestic violence in the churches and communities with large minority populations. Since Pastor Walker had already agreed to hold the planning meeting at the church, the church felt obligated to honor the engagement.

Trying hard to garner some new support in the church and at the same time have her name illuminated in a positive light in the community, Lulabelle decided to take on the project. She coordinated the effort by meeting with thirty female volunteers immediately after Sunday morning worship the next weekend. She asked the volunteers to deliver pamphlets and hang signs, and before she could even go into her speech, the volunteers had already grabbed the pamphlets and signs, then took their seats. Lulabelle then announced that she had already coordinated public service messages that were being posted on billboards, advertised in the local and community newspapers, and announced the event on local radio stations. Deacon Evans sat proudly as he grinned and watched Lulabelle speak before the gathered group of volunteers. However, Lena Hobson, One Way's poster child for domestic violence, rolled her eyes at Lulabelle and mumbled the word "Hypocrite," oblivious to the startled stares and Deacon Evans' frown directed toward her.

For the first time in One Way history, members were actually enthusiastic about being a part of a project managed by Lulabelle. The members' response to this project even took Lulabelle by surprise. She was certain that she would receive a lot of resistance, and a small turnout. However, self-doubt was removed when she saw all the members gathered to hear instructions about the project.

Lulabelle stood before the volunteers and shouted, "Praise God for all of the volunteers gathered to help with eradicating domestic violence in our church and community." Lulabelle then went through a list of tasks that required volunteers. As she looked at the teenagers, she asked if they would volunteer to distribute pamphlets and post signs in neighborhoods on the south side of town. They giggled as they agreed to canvass neighborhoods.

Clearing her throat, Mother Kellie looked at the teenagers. "Young ladies, domestic violence is a serious matter, and we are so glad that you all want to be involved in this mission ... right, Lulabelle?"

A stunned Lulabelle replied, "Yes, ma'am. Mother Kellie, you are so right. So we'll all meet back here this Saturday for the workshop, okay?"

Early that Saturday morning Lulabelle arrived at the church in time to meet the caterer she'd personally hired to prepare food for the meeting. Lulabelle had always passed herself off as a great soul food cook, but very few knew that she couldn't cook. She always hired someone to bake a cake or fry some chicken whenever she volunteered to bring a covered dish to a church function. So she showed up four hours before the domestic violence planning meeting and luncheon to allow the caterer access to the church for delivery and setup. The caterer, Soul Food Delights, knew Lulabelle liked to keep her business on the down-low. Mary Benson, Soul Food Delights' owner, arrived in an unmarked truck at the rear entrance of the church. Mrs. Benson knew the routine. She would bring the oil she used to fry the chicken and set it up in one of Lulabelle's pots, then place it on the church stove. She would then throw all of the trash in the kitchen's garbage can. She would leave all of the ingredients she used to cook the food on the countertop in the kitchen, so that when it was time to clean up the kitchen and members volunteered to help, it would appear that Lulabelle had been cooking all morning for the meeting.

On the other side of town, Mother Kellie was picking up Lena Dobson, who was sporting a swollen nose and busted lip. Lena had been with her abusive boyfriend, Ray, for more than eight years. Pastor Walker had been counseling her to get professional help. Mother Kellie thought by volunteering and asking Lena to come along and assist, she could open Lena's eyes to the seriousness of domestic violence. Folks from the church and her family had been talking to Lena, but Mother Kellie hoped that hearing another's story might hit home for Lena.

Lena hopped into Mother Kellie's black Corvette, and Mother Kellie leaned over to give her a hug.

"Lena, thank you for coming with me. I hope we have a great turnout for this meeting."

"No problem, Mother Kellie. I am always willing to help my church family."

"Lena, I need to ask you a question. I know that Pastor Walker had been counseling you before he left the church. However, I need to know, was there anything else going on between you and Pastor Walker?"

Lena shook her head and responded, "Absolutely not! Pastor Walker provided me a listening ear and shoulder to cry on. He was like the father I never had. Where did you get this story? I bet it was that nosey next door neighbor of his. If she had a man, she wouldn't be in Pastor Walker's business."

Mother Kellie raised a hand. "Lena, calm down."

"Pastor Walker and me! That is so ridiculous."

"I am sorry, but I needed to ask. Ms. Roxie mentioned she saw you leaving Pastor Walker's home early one morning. We must examine all leads."

"Whatever, Mother Kellie."

As the members began arriving at church, they were greeted with the smell of freshly brewed coffee. Entering the fellowship hall, they saw that Lulabelle had put out a spread that consisted of lemon pound cake, sweet potato pie, potato salad, homemade rolls, and fried chicken wings. When the members heard that Lulabelle, alone, had prepared all of the food, many of them just rolled their eyes.

Lulabelle greeted each member with a hug and a seemingly gracious "Thank you for coming."

As the ladies, young and old, began taking their seats, Lulabelle announced that they were expecting twenty staff members from the shelter to go over the planning and schedule for next week's events. She expressed gratitude to everyone for keeping their promises to help, despite Pastor Walker's departure.

Lulabelle extended a formal welcome and presented a brief history of One Way. She then turned the meeting over to the shelter's training director, Shelley Kamacho, a tall, thin white woman with the prettiest blue eyes. Shelley got all hyped up speaking about domestic violence. Once Shelley finished her speech, she introduced the next speaker from the shelter: a hard-looking black woman named Abby Otts.

Abby was the outreach director for the shelter, and because all the One Way Church volunteers were African American, Shelley felt it would be better for Abby to address them. A six-foot-tall woman who must have weighed 275 pounds, Abby looked as if she could hold her own. But after starting her story, it was clear that she had once been a victim of domestic violence. Abby shared how her abuse began as a push or a pointing of a finger in her face, then it progressed to a slap, and then it eventually led to daily beatings. "I had to go to work with black eyes, busted lips, a busted nose, and bruises on my head."

Abby paused, then told the group, "As a child I watched my mom drop everything and everybody for a man, and she was just desperate to keep a man at all costs. I remember as a child watching my mom get beaten so badly before she went to work. Momma would take her beating out on us kids. I remember one time when Momma came to pick up me, my brother, and sister from our aunt's house. Our aunt pleaded with her to leave her abuser. My siblings and I were hoping and praying momma would take the help because we were on edge all the time. With two black eyes, my momma told my aunt, 'I rather have any man than no man.' My aunt shook her head in disbelief as momma grabbed us and took us home by bus. My mother ended up marrying the jerk, and there were fewer beatings as he got older and slower—and as we kids got older and bigger, we wouldn't allow him to hit our momma."

As Abby went on with her story, Lena began sobbing in the arms of Mother Kellie.

Mother Kellie shoved tissues into Lena's hand and whispered into her ear, "Baby, sometimes God uses others to open our eyes. Now dry up so we can hear the rest of Abby's testimony."

"Yes, ma'am," Lena replied as she dried her eyes.

Meanwhile Abby went on. "I vowed that when I graduated high school, I was going to move and be free from fighting and cursing. But I fell to the same demon. I started picking up any man that smiled my way. I would move him in and take care of him, only to watch him take advantage of me and leave me. Then for some crazy reason I believed if I got pregnant, they would stay and not beat me. Boy, was I wrong. I would get slapped, pushed, stood up, cursed out, and left all the time. Even after kicking them out of my home, I would welcome them back with open arms. Eight kids later and eight baby daddies later, I was still doing the same thing. I was the greatest catch to an abuser. I got over $1,000 a month in food stamps. I got over $600 a month in child support. My housing was free and I worked part-time. I would put a man before my own kids. I couldn't drive, and never went anywhere because I always needed a babysitter, and who would be willing to babysit eight kids at one time? I wasn't street smart, so anything a man told me, I would believe. Foolish, I was.

"My last abuser brainwashed me into believing he was the only man for me. He was the only one who loved me. I would never find another man like him in this world. He convinced me we were soul mates. He told me he was going to marry me and be a father to all of my kids. When I told my grandmother my good news, she said, 'Where is the engagement ring? Are you nuts to fall for this crap again?' Sadly I didn't listen to what she was trying to tell me. He worked, but I never saw his money, although he always had access to my money. He had a car, but my kids and I were never allowed to ride in it. When I needed groceries, I would struggle on the bus or have a relative to take me to the store. When my lights, phone, or cable got disconnected, he was never around until I got them reconnected. My family finally gave up on me and only called to check on the kids."

As Abby proceeded with her story, there were tears all through the audience. Many saw themselves, friends, and family members in her testimony. To hear Abby confess the many years of abuse she had endured felt so painful. All the while, Lulabelle was working the audience, distributing tissues to the teary-eyed folks.

Abby kept going. "My family always told me I should leave. How? Where would I go with eight kids? I remember one night after me and my kids got beat up, my uncle came and got us. Although he complained about the bed bugs and roaches we brought with us, and my kids' unruly behavior, he opened his home to us. However, once he found out I was talking to my abuser and meeting him after work, he put me out.

"He said, 'After all I went through bringing you and your eight hard-headed kids into my home, and after that no good son of a gun beat the crap out of you and these kids, you turn around and take him back. Fine. Pack up your stuff, because I am taking you back to where you want to be. Go home!'

"I shouted, 'I don't have no lights. What am I supposed to do?'

"My uncle said, 'Not my problem.'" Abby paused, then continued. "After that my abuser drilled into my head how my family meant me no good and how he was the only one there for me and my kids. He kept saying that his job was stressing him out and that was why he kept hitting on me. He said he was working it out and was not going to do it again. Of course, that only lasted for a couple of weeks.

"I watched my kids get beat up trying to defend me. I remember two of my daughters going to school with a black eye. I had to drill them to say they got into a fight with each other. That man had me so sprung, that I had my kids lying to protect him."

No one in the audience moved, and dead silence reigned as Abby went on. "It was my low self-esteem that made it possible for me to stay in this violent relationship for more than five years. The final straw was when my abuser bought a gun and threatened my oldest son by putting the gun to his head if he didn't turn over his Christmas money that his father had given him. The next day set off a series of events, starting with my eldest son telling his teacher what happened. The teacher called his father. Then, when I was called to the school, I had just endured a beating and I had to lie to the administrators. When the administrators took one look at me and listened to the lie I told, they called the state and the police. All of my children were temporarily removed from my home the week before Christmas. Counselor after counselor kept telling me to stop making excuses for this man, who cared nothing about me, because the abuse I was subjecting my kids to was even worse and could cause them a lifetime of emotional problems. By the time I mustered up the courage to leave, the state had officially removed my children and placed them with their fathers. At this point I was ordered to pay child support and was granted supervised visitation. Many of you are probably thinking that is when I cleaned my life up, right? Wrong! I stayed with the jerk another year, and yeah, I didn't pay child support nor visit with my kids. I was pretty stupid. After my family blamed me for losing my kids and started to look down on me and put me down, he was the only comfort to me.

"Then one night when we were out at a local supper club, I noticed him talking to a white female up at the bar. He had just told me he was going to the men's room, so I was hopping mad. Here I am paying for the gas to get us here, paying for the meal, paid for the clothes, shoes, and jewelry he wearing, and he going to disrespect me by talking to some white girl! I was mad. So I stormed up there with my lip poked out and puffed-up cheeks and jumped into the female's face, telling her to leave my man alone. When he saw the scene I was making, he gently tapped me on my shoulder. When I turned to see what he wanted, he punched me in my nose, which sent me to the floor, bleeding. Then he kicked me. The white female he was talking to pushed him off of me and told him to stop. I was shocked by her courage. She stood there with him towering over her, and dared him to hit her. I thought to myself, *She is nuts.* You know what? He backed down. He looked up at her and called her a bitch. She then grabbed her mace from her purse and told him if he touched me again, she was going to spray him unconscious. Then she shouted for someone to call 9-1-1, and he left running.

"As we were waiting for the police to arrive, she came to me and asked me if I was all right, and I told her yes. I then told her I was sorry for being so hateful. She looked at me and asked how many years he had been abusing me. I asked her how she knew. She said, 'I am an abuse counselor; I know the signs. By the way, my name is Shelley, and I am going to make it my business to make sure that you never endure domestic violence ever again. Will you trust me?'

"She was very smart and intelligent about domestic violence. As she spoke, she stared into my eyes, and I felt like she was sent from God to rescue me from this mess I was sinking deep into. I watched Shelley move to get me ice, and she held my hand when the police took her statement. Tears flowed all the way down to my lips as I refused to press charges, but Shelley had no problem providing the police with my abuser's information. She gave them my abuser's name, phone number, make and model of the car he was driving, and she as a witness gave them the entire story. She also told them that he might be staying at my house, and that I would be staying with her until he was apprehended.

"As I was being treated for a black eye, Shelley sat with me and continued to hold my hand. She kept telling me that I deserved to be treated like a lady, and not an animal. She kept saying how much of a loser my abuser was because he hit a woman. She then began to wipe the tears from my eyes and said, 'Honey, there is no way in hell I am going to let you go back to that loser.' Ten other people in the restaurant corroborated her story. That night she allowed me to stay at her house. The next morning she took me back to my place and helped me to get settled. All I could say to her was thank you and how sorry I was. Before she left, I asked her why she felt so obligated to do all of this for me. She looked at me and simply said, 'You are my sister. I am just as guilty as your abuser if I do nothing but watch him beat you.'"

Abby shook her head and said, "Friends, I never got my kids back because I needed healing and counseling, as did my children. My children were receiving counseling during the time I was still out there in denial. I did not want to interrupt their stable lives. So I continued in counseling for two years and graduated college. Today I am a born- again Christian and licensed social worker. I have repaired my relationship with all eight of my children. I have two children in college and the others reside with their fathers. I see my children every other weekend, and I play an active role in their education. I have been fortunate to maintain my friendship with Shelley, who has been my employer for the last five years. Shelley saved my life by introducing me to Christ and helping me find myself. Friends, join us as we try to save more women from the brutal hands of domestic violence."

Before Abby could take her seat, a thunderous applause arose from around the room. Even Lulabelle rose from her seat to give Abby a standing ovation. Having periodically made eye contact with Lena throughout her testimony, Abby now made her way to the back of the fellowship hall and gave Lena a huge hug. She told her, "You have the rest of your life to be away from the jerk you are crying about, and the domestic violence, but the choice is yours. Here is my card. Anytime you want to talk, just call me. Sister, it's up to you to make the first step. You must stop suffering and stop the suffering of your family."

After everyone had settled down and finished wiping their tears, the women broke into groups for each stage of the conference. Meanwhile Lena met in the Mothers' Room with Abby. They talked for several hours.

The setup in the fellowship hall consisted of ten tables with lavender tablecloths, topped with brochures, paperwork, pitchers of sweet tea, and plates of cake and chicken wings. Seated at the tables were women of varied races—planning, laughing, discussing, and learning about domestic violence. Standing and observing this sight, Lulabelle beamed with pride and uneasy feelings. As she stood in the corner, with tears streaming down from her eyes, Shelley darted up to her and comforted her with, "Now, honey, you don't have to be abused anymore. You can come to the shelter tonight if you are afraid to go home."

Lulabelle looked up at Shelley, tucked and tilted her chin down toward her neck, and asked, "Are you talking to me? Apparently signals have been crossed. My husband is the head deacon of this church, and he would never harm me, so you need to keep it moving."

Shelley took two steps back and said, "Sweetie, the shelter is open twenty-four hours, so when you are ready to talk, we will be waiting." Shelley then tossed her long blonde hair over her right shoulder and returned to her table.

After the meeting adjourned, everyone fixed to-go plates before they departed. As Mother Kellie drove Lena home, Lena leaned over to Mother Kellie, touched her shoulder, and said, "Mother Kellie, thank you for encouraging me to come today. I have truly been inspired and blessed. This not only gave me some hope, but a plan of action to get out of my mess."

"Lena, I am glad this gave you some hope. Just know, hope is good but it can be painful."

Soon Mother Kellie pulled up to Lena's home, and she told her, "Baby, take care of yourself and stay prayerful. Thank you for coming with me today. See you tomorrow."

Lena waved as she was inserting her key into the door. Mother Kellie tooted the horn and headed home.

THE MEETING

At the first One Way Senior 11 Committee meeting, all the committee members were present and looking sharp on a sunny Saturday morning. The deacons sat together on one side of the table while the mothers sat on the opposite side. The other committee members were scattered in between. Brother Mason and Miss Lillian were also present, along with a dozen or so members who sat along the edges of the room, having come to observe as Brother Mason had said was allowed when he told them about the Senior 11 Committee.

Since no one was sure about how the meeting should start, Brother Mason took the lead by asking the committee, "How soon would you like to have the new pastor installed?"

Turning the question back to him, Deacon Evans asked, "Brother Mason, what do you recommend?"

With all eyes fixed on him, Brother Mason said, "I would recommend that we have a pastor named prior to our upcoming church anniversary, and that would mean we name a pastor within sixty days. Mothers, I realize your cruise is forthcoming, so we can begin advertising now so that by the time you return, all resumes will have been received."

"Thank you, Brother Mason, for considering our obligations," Mother Kellie said with a gentle smile.

In a bitter voice, and with a twitch of his nose, Deacon Evans asked, "Mother, what's the priority here: your cruise or the church?"

Still upset about the pastor-wanted ad placed by Deacon Evans' wife, Mother Kellie stared into the eyes of Deacon Evans and said, "Excuse me?"

"I didn't' stutter," Deacon Evans said.

Mother Kellie shifted in her chair to face Deacon Evans. "How dare you question the mothers' commitment to One Way, after you stood before the membership and lied about wanting to include the members in the hiring process and then went behind our backs and advertised the position anyway! Then you come into this meeting this morning and try to divert attention from your own devious and unholy behavior and try to put the focus on the mothers. You are an evil old man, Deacon Evans."

The mothers began to scoot their chairs back from the table. They knew Deacon Evans should back off, because Mother Kellie had no problem debating with the best of them.

Of course his stubborn nature wouldn't allow him to say nothing, and he replied, "Woman, what are you driving at?"

Mother Kellie stood up and pounded her fist on the table. "I am driving at your cruel motive to rush and name a new pastor, ignoring the church's feelings and policy. Do you have something to hide? Maybe you and that wife of yours know what really happened to Pastor Walker? Don't even think for a moment that we, the Mothers' Board, are fools." Mother Kellie moved directly in front of Deacon Evans' face, looked him in his eyes, and said, "I will personally skin you like a Lake Erie catfish if I ever find out you had anything to do with Pastor Walker's disappearance. Mark my words, Deacon Evans."

As Mother Kellie went back to her seat, a genuinely baffled Deacon Evans asked, "What are you talking about?" He then looked around at the other members at the table and asked, "What is she talking about?"

In an effort to diffuse the situation, Mother Mae calmly told Deacon Evans, "The religious empowerment cruise that the mothers are booked on is open to the public. We have no problem if other church auxiliaries decide to come along."

As Mother Kellie regained her composure, a now shaking and sweating Deacon Evans excused himself to get a glass of water.

Brother Mason quickly moved the conversation to explaining the details of the process: "Committee members, I will write and advertise a professional position description for the vacant pastor position. I will make sure the position is advertised in several newspapers and religious periodicals for a period of ten days. Upon the closing date of the position, I will assemble and copy all of the resumes, along with the professional references, and forward copies to each committee member. Based on the number of qualified resumes, Miss Lillian will coordinate an on-site interview and church visit. The final plan is to have the top candidates return to interview, and conduct Sunday school and preach Sunday-morning service to allow the congregation to get a feel for each candidate. Then the membership will vote on the candidate they feel is most qualified to lead One Way."

Once the committee agreed on the process, the meeting was adjourned. As the committee members were getting their coats, Deacon Evans, still scratching his head and feeling lost, approached Mother Kellie and said, "Mother Kellie, I am sorry if my actions offended you."

In a sincere tone Mother Kellie answered, "Your actions did offend me. The words you speak mean absolutely nothing to me. When your actions begin to speak louder than your words, I will be ready to forgive you." Mother Kellie turned to drape her sweater over her shoulders. "Deacon Evans, you have not only disrespected the Mothers' Board, but One Way."

Deacon Evans looked into Mother Kellie's eyes. "I am going to work hard to win you over, Mother Kellie, because I saw the hurt in your eyes and heard it in your voice."

Mother Kellie said nothing and remained resolute.

As Deacon Evans departed, Mother Kellie stood and watched him leave. For the first time someone had crawled underneath his skin and gone blow for blow with him. Mother Kellie hadn't stuttered or hesitated; she had stared him in his eyes and hadn't compromised her stance.

During his ride home Deacon Evans was thinking, *Just who she think she was talking to me like that? I should have gotten that old hag told, but I had to be a gentleman about this mess. That's all right; I'll get the last laugh on this one.*

As the mothers congregated in the Mothers' Room, some of the mothers asked Mother Kellie what she and Deacon Evans were whispering about in the corner. Mother Kellie told them, "He offered me an apology, and I flatly refused to accept it. I told him that when his actions begin to speak louder than his words, I will forgive him."

Mother Mae asked, "Wouldn't it have been Christ-like to forgive Deacon Evans?"

"Absolutely," Mother Kellie said.

"Huh? Then why didn't you accept that man's apology?" asked Mother Addie.

Mother Kellie looked around. "Mothers, Deacon Evans is arrogant. He knows that he will be forgiven every time for every misdeed, whether intentional or unintentional. I was tired of looking the other way and allowing him to think that he can say and do anything and not feel any remorse. Now I feel better, so much better."

"Well," Mother Addie said, "I never saw that man look so scared. Mother Kellie, I think you got him afraid."

Mother Kellie shook her head and smiled. "He's like the Terminator: he will be back—stronger and slicker come next week. I do believe there is some good in that man, I surely do. Right now it's our job to rid the devil from him."

The mothers began talking and getting excited about their upcoming five-day cruise, counting down the days until they embarked.

Meanwhile Lulabelle was working on Deacon Evans' plan to get back at the mothers for their interference. She blamed them for delaying the hiring of One Way's next pastor. After a long night of plotting on how to get under their skin, she came up with what she thought was a brilliant plan. The deacons and Miss Lillian, the church secretary, would accompany the mothers on the "Empowering the Church" cruise. Even with the last-minute notice, she knew their presence would irritate the mothers. Deacon Evans was not comfortable with this plan, as he was really conflicted about doing better, but Lulabelle and her womanly ways got the best of him.

Once the news circulated among the congregation that the deacon board would be going on the cruise, the mothers called an emergency meeting. Deacon King told the mothers that the rumors they had heard about the deacons and Miss Lillian joining them on the cruise were true, and not to despair because this conference might actually do some good for the deacons. Mother Mae told the mothers it would give them some bonding time with the other deacons and Miss Lillian. She emphasized that Miss Lillian had never been on a vacation and this would be good for her. The other mothers reluctantly bought into the idea, but they felt like their time was being invaded by this unwelcome intrusion. They did seem pleased to know that Miss Lillian felt truly excited about coming along on the retreat. Mother Mae reassured the mothers that the deacons' and Miss Lillian's trip would be paid for via their own respective budgets, and the mothers would not be responsible for any of their expenses.

Deacon Evans called Mother Mae and asked for the mothers' flight information, as the deacons and Miss Lillian wished to fly together with the mothers. Mother Mae graciously provided Deacon Evans with the information. Unbeknownst to Deacon Evans, the mothers' hefty auxiliary account balance allowed them to fly first class and upgrade their cruise cabins to suites.

THE CRUISE

Miss Lillian and the deacons were among the last passengers to board the large MD-88 aircraft headed to Miami, Florida. As the deacons entered the aircraft and walked through the first-class cabin, they observed the mothers relaxing and drinking champagne in their sumptuous seats. As Deacon Evans moved through the first-class cabin, he pretended not to see the mothers, but the mothers made sure all the deacons noticed them as they walked through their section.

During the three-hour nonstop flight to Miami, Deacon Evans was squeezed between two hefty salesmen who reeked of menthol cigarettes, beer, and onions. Every chance he got, he made his way to the restroom in the first-class cabin. On the fourth occasion the flight attendant tapped his shoulder and advised him to use the restroom at the rear of the plane, as the one in first class was intended only for first-class passengers. When Deacon Evans nodded and said he'd be quick, another flight attendant arrived on the scene, blocked Deacon Evans' access to the restroom, and pointed him back to the coach section. Deacon Evans gave the flight attendant a disdainful look as he motioned for her to step aside, and then he made his way to the rear of the plane. Mother Millie giggled and waved at Deacon Evans as he was booted from the first-class cabin.

Once the plane landed and all the passengers had retrieved their luggage from the baggage claim carousel, the mothers' Cadillac Escalade stretch limousine arrived to take them to the port. They graciously offered Miss Lillian and the deacons a ride, which they gladly accepted, except for Deacons Evans and Carter, whose pride prevented them from accepting the tempting offer. Deacons Evans and Carter opted to wait for the cruise-line shuttle bus. Once the shuttle bus arrived, Deacon Evans and Carter boarded the over-crowded vehicle that had no working air-conditioning and no available seats. They had to stand the duration of the fifteen-minute ride from the airport to the cruise port. By the time they arrived at the port, they both were a hot, sweaty mess.

With priority boarding status on the cruise line, the mothers got right into their cabins. Miss Lillian and the deacons waited more than an hour before reaching their cabins. The deacons were less than pleased with their accommodations, as they were confined to an interior cabin with no windows and two bunk beds. Deacon King refused to bunk with his assigned group, and he pleaded with Miss Lillian and Mother Mae to help him out, anxious to see whether they had any extra room. Miss Lillian, of course, refused Deacon King. The mothers, who were two to a suite, offered one of their suites to four of the deacons. The suite would easily accommodate four men. Deacon King and two other deacons graciously thanked the mothers and began gathering their belongings from the cramped cabin. Deacon Evans, of course, would not take the suite accommodations offered by the mothers, and called the deacons who did "wimps."

As he was gathering his belongings, Deacon King responded to Deacon Evans, "Yes, wimps we may be, but plenty of space we will have." The suites were equipped with wet bars, a living room, a deck, and a bedroom with two double beds. The living room had a sleeper sofa.

The mothers made their way down to the formal dining room for dinner. The sequins and diamonds coming from their table were blinding to the cameras that snapped photos at nearby tables. The mothers relished the attention. By the time 11:00 p.m. rolled around, some of the mothers were nodding off at the table, while others were soaking up the atmosphere of lively conversations and music all about the restaurant. After leaving the restaurant, the mothers stopped in the casino and tried their luck on the penny slots.

The mothers returned to their suites around midnight and turned in, to be ready for their classes in the morning. As she set the alarm on her nightstand, Mother Janie asked Mother Millie, "Oh my Lord, you reckon we will be able to make tomorrow morning's class on time?"

The next morning the blinding sunshine gazed down over the pretty blue Caribbean Sea as the mothers struggled to get out of bed. Deacon Evans and the other deacons had already eaten breakfast and were at the first scheduled training class for the day. By the time the mothers were up and ready, they decided they would be too late for their morning session, but would make their afternoon seminars.

Once they arrived in the training room that afternoon, they saw they were the first to show. They signed in and headed for the front table in the first row. The other attendees arrived, eventually filling the room to capacity, and the mothers were good to go.

The instructor stood before the class and introduced himself. He was a minister from Salt Lake City, Utah—Reverend Sammie Morris.

Mother Janie scrunched her eyebrows and shook her head. She whispered to Mother Millie, "I didn't know they had black folks up in Utah. Just don't seem like a state with black folks."

Mother Millie laughed and said, "Child, we are everywhere."

The instructor was speaking on "Morale in the Church." Reverend Morris jumped right into his presentation, asking, "Class, are you aware that one person is able to infect an entire congregation—able to kill the morale of an entire organization? If that infection is not dealt with promptly, it will spread and infect the rest of the body. End result, death."

When the mothers heard that, Pastor Walker immediately came to their minds, along with the positive changes he had been trying to implement and the resistance he had faced. The mothers began taking detailed notes as they listened to Reverend Morris.

At the end of Reverend Morris' message, he asked for questions, so Mother Kellie raised her hand.

Reverend Morris read her name badge and said, "Yes, Mother Kellie?"

"How can church members aid in killing the infection once its location has been identified?"

Reverend Morris raised his glasses from his eyes onto his head to get a closer glimpse of Mother Kellie and determine if she was sincere. He told her, "Pray and go to the person with the infection, and go into prayer together. Talk to your sister or brother and find out their trouble. They just might need someone to talk to, or they might not even be aware. The ice must be broken."

"Thank you kindly, Reverend Morris," said Mother Kellie. She frowned, none too happy with the answer.

Another student from the back of the classroom asked, "Reverend Morris, the morale in our church is at an all-time low because we have a great deal of division between the members that got it going on and those that don't. In addition we are having difficulty with unruly children and disrespectful and bored teens in our church. Could you please offer us some advice?"

Reverend Morris walked back to the podium, deep in thought, with his thumb on his chin and responded, "Be thankful you are living to see a rough patch and able to ask for help to get through it. Many folks have stumbled and given up, but that should never be a characteristic of God's church. Don't let the devil steal your joy. When you are concerned about what other people think and how they see you, you are opening the door to the devil. God always looks at our hearts. Too often, people get consumed with appearance. I can't tell you how many good-looking, classy-dressing, nice-car-driving folks have made a quick exit to death by being too consumed with self.

When you look at an obituary, they never mention how beautiful or fly someone was—or how someone only carried designer handbags and drove luxury cars. They normally speak to the person's character and heart, because that carries more weight. God don't put more on us than we can bear. I have heard and seen it all. But what I find most disgraceful is how our children are being raised. Parents dropping them off, parents substituting things for time spent with their children, and grandparents and other family members looking the other way because they don't want to be bothered or offend anyone. It truly takes an entire family, including the church, to raise and mold a child. It's way too easy to have a baby; the work is in the rearing and development of the child. Children don't know anything about video games, designer clothes, shoes, money, drugs, and alcohol until they are taught. What would the black community be if we taught our children love, family values, self-respect, nonviolence, how to manage money, how to speak up for yourself, how to look folks in the eye when you talk, math, English, science, foreign languages, peace, strength, and on and on?"

Bursts of "Amen," "Hallelujah," and "Preach, brother" were shouted from the audience.

"We would have the colleges bursting with eager learners instead of the prisons overcrowded with hardened criminals!" Reverend Morris said.

As the classroom erupted in a long applause, Reverend Morris indicated that time was up, and thanked everyone for their attention and participation.

Mother Janie asked whether Reverend Morris conducted on-site workshops, and he told her he would love to. After the seminar the mothers collected Reverend Morris' contact information and told him they would be in touch. The mothers felt this seminar was the start of a wonderful Christ-centered cruise.

That evening the mothers relaxed in chaise lounges on the top deck of the ship while watching a breathtaking sunset. As the cruise ship sailed into the night, the mothers chatted about their children, and of course about their beloved One Way. The mothers cried as much as they laughed as they reminisced about how God had blessed each of them over the years. They gave praises to God that none of them had been inflicted with disease, and that they were all in their right minds.

The ocean breeze wafted across their faces and hair, which eased the mothers into a more relaxed state. The mothers' loud laughs shifted to loud snores, and they were soon fast asleep. Eventually a crewmember awakened them and helped the mothers up from their chairs. They joked and laughed all the way back to their cabins.

The next morning delivered gorgeous blue skies over the turquoise tint of the ocean as the ship headed to Aruba. The mothers felt excitement while getting ready for the next seminar, "Games People Play in the Church." Again, the mothers were the first to arrive and claimed the front-row seats, but the room quickly filled to capacity. The deacons managed to get the last row of seats. When the minister, Reverend Bernie Hall from Chicago, walked into the room, he immediately complimented the mothers on their cruise attire and said how happy he was to see everyone. The mothers enjoyed the compliment so much that they sat a little taller and gave Reverend Hall their full attention. Reverend Hall displayed a warm, yet confident demeanor.

He said, "We all know church folks that play games to get their bills paid and how they scam to take the church's money. People, we as stewards ... we as Christians must stand for what is right and stop looking the other way. What are we teaching our children? Are we teaching them that the church is a cash cow and that we have trees planted behind the church that bear dollar bills?"

"Say it, brother!" Mother Janie shouted.

The other mothers nodded.

Reverend Hall continued, "What message are we sending?"

Mother Janie whispered to Mother Kellie, "That's Clara Mae."

"Sure you right," said Mother Kellie.

Reverend Hall then spoke about how the church had unholy folks in positions the leaders knew they weren't spiritually and mentally qualified to handle. "Folks, how are you going to have a deacon lead-ing devotional service when he can't stand the pastor or the ushers? He irritates half of the membership and feels he and his family are the only ones in the church with class. His wife and children are out of control. His entire family has an attitude problem. Just because he has a set of keys to the church's front door and the alarm code, he and his family think they own the church."

From the audience came laughter and shouts of "Amen!"

While the other deacons from One Way thought this was funny, Deacon Evans shifted in his seat, folded his arms, and crossed his legs as he checked his watch.

Reverend Hall continued, "You've seen this deacon, when pastor is preaching, he is looking at his watch and turning from the front pew to the rear of the church to check the clock. After benediction he's not leaving the sanctuary—because he is already in his car pull-ing out of the church's driveway!"

Nods and more laughter came from the audience. Meanwhile Deacon Evans yawned.

Reverend Hall went on. "Let's talk about the ushers. They are the gatekeepers of God's house. They are the first people you see when entering the house of worship. They have to be punctual. Godly. Warm." As Reverend Hall walked back to the front of the conference room, he turned and said, "However, we know ushers who ignore church members will certainly ignore visitors. Don't be fooled."

Reverend Hall peeked over the top of his glasses as he smiled, while the audience was nodding and applauding.

"Have you ever wondered why visitors aren't coming back? Check your ushers out. Instead of greeting visitors with a smile, they are rolling their eyes at the visitors, sighing, or outright ignoring the visi-tors. Visitors can't get a bulletin, Bible, or a hymnal book. However, when you and I come in with our Bible and hymnal in hand, the ush-ers are forcing us to take another hymnal and Bible. These are the same books they couldn't find last week when we had visitors. Some of our ushers are asleep while standing and sitting on the job. When you need a fan or a tissue, the ushers are nowhere to be found. Don't raise your hand to get the usher's attention. That's a sure way to be ignored. Can I get a witness?"

Many in the audience offered verbal agreement, along with nodding their heads.

Reverend Hall paused and took off his glasses. "Seriously, folks," he continued. "Our ushers hold an important job and we have to make sure we have the right people at the door. You don't want an argumentative and combative person at the church's door. Someone with untreated bipolar disorder or in anger management treatment class for the third time should not be on the usher board. Think about it. We need some friendly and smiling faces at the door. Just think, what type of face would you like to be greeted by when you get to heaven? For many people in the streets, the church is heaven on earth to them. We need to make them feel welcome."

Most of the audience rose to its feet, praising the Lord. The reverend then talked about working together—setting aside egos, letting go of how things have been done for years, and working together to embrace positive changes for the church.

As Reverend Hall moved to the front row, where the mothers were seated, he continued. "It's so hard to embrace change when you are old because you have to learn new things. Many people aren't willing to give their elders a chance to learn or catch up. We are often discredited because we move a little slower, it takes us a minute more to comprehend discussion points, or our gray hair is a distraction."

As Reverend Hall carried on, tears began to stream down some of the mothers' faces. For the first time in many years, the mothers were beginning to feel like a hindrance to their beloved One Way. Once Reverend Hall got a glimpse of some of the mothers wiping tears, he backed up to their table, read one of their name badges, and said, "Mother Mae, talk to me. What are you feeling right now?"

She sniffled, then said, "As the senior mother at my church, I often feel as if the younger members make the elders feel worthless because they move a little slower, take a little longer to comprehend or respond to their questions, and we are not on top of technology and new Christian ideas. I admit, I am old school, and it does take me a while to embrace change, but once I do, I give it my heart and I hate being categorized as almost dead, because I am so full of life. These are the games I don't like being played on me or any of my sisters and brothers in Christ."

Reverend Hall asked Mother Mae to come up front and stand before the class. He walked around Mother Mae and stared at her from head to toe.

"Mother, I perceive you to be a strong, God-fearing woman who is shaping the women at her church, in her community, and in her family. Am I right?"

"I am doing my very best."

"So what if you move a little slower? We will get to the same place. So what if your brain computes a little slower? We will get to the same answer. The folks that play these types of games are evil, jealous, intimidated, and unholy. God has granted you a full life. You have been an obedient servant, and God is going to continue blessing you. God speaks favorably about our church elders. Mother Mae, thank you for coming up here. Please take your seat."

As she did so, Reverend Hall said, "Class, pull out your Bibles, because we are going to give Mother Mae something to shout about this morning. Let's go to Psalm 107:32, and then we'll move to Proverbs 31:23, Acts 14:23, and Hebrews 11:2."

Reverend Hall moved from one scripture to another, all of them speaking about "elders," and the mothers' enthusiasm grew. The reverend read each scripture with authority and praise. He then kept the mothers' excited by saying, "Mother Mae, you have nothing to feel bad about. If you are at a Bible-teaching church, then your pastor has already told the deacons, choir, ushers, missionaries, and any other organization at your church that the elders are a part of God's divine plan. Your pastor has told them that disrespecting the elders and mothers of the church will not be tolerated by anyone—no matter your position or the amount of your tithes."

Miss Lillian turned and pointed back to Deacon Evans. He responded by scratching his nose with his middle finger. Eyes slit, Miss Lillian waved her fist at Deacon Evans. He rolled his eyes, then waved her to the back of the room and mouthed the words, "Bring it."

As Reverend Hall preached on in a thunderous voice, Mother Mae shouted "Hallelujah!" several times. Reverend Hall came over, touched her shoulder, and said, "When that walk gets heavier and those young hard-headed game-playing folks at your church think they have nailed your coffin shut, you tell them that Jesus got up off that cross! You tell them that when Abraham was counted out, God stopped the count and stepped up Abraham's game and allowed Sarah to bear him a son!" Reverend Hall began striding around the perimeter of the room, then shouted to Mother Mae, "You tell them to take a good look at those obituaries; weekly, the young are outnumbering the old. And there is a strong—hear me, Mother Mae—a strong possibility that you will be singing at their funerals if they don't get right with God."

Reverend Hall pulled out his handkerchief and dabbed the sweat from his head as he chuckled. Meanwhile Mother Mae had gotten to her feet, bobbing her head from side to side while clapping.

"They don't know who they are dealing with," the reverend continued. "Mother Mae, you continue to hold your head high. Believe it or not, the church needs more strong, God-fearing mothers like you and your crew, because these young folks don't know how to act; they don't know how to be parents; they don't know what hard work is. They are busy scamming and scheming. They want a quick fix, instant gratification—the real world that you and I know, it don't work like that. These parents want to be friends with their kids, they want their kids to express themselves, they want to be perceived as cool to their kids, but when these kids get older and start disrespecting and abusing them, it's too late. We need better examples. We need better deacons, we need better choir members, and we need church leaders with the total package. Not Sunday-only Christians; we need every-day-of-my-life Christians. We need more long-term members, more stability, more love in our churches. Who better to teach it and show it than the elder church members?"

As Reverend Hall wiped the sweat from his forehead again, he said, "Class, I didn't come here to preach today, but the Lord used me to help Mother Mae and maybe someone else up in here."

Mother Mae took her seat, knowing that the word had just been for her and the mothers. As she looked around her table, she saw the other mothers wiping tears and caught up in the Spirit. At the conclusion of Reverend Hall's seminar, the mothers collected his contact information and told him they would be in touch.

When the mothers departed the classroom, they agreed they hadn't been moved like that since Pastor Walker's last sermon. They all felt Reverend Hall was special, and he even reminded them of Pastor Walker.

On the final day of the cruise, the mothers attended the "Not What You Say, But How You Say It" seminar. Again they were the first to arrive, but immediately after they took their seats, the deacons and Miss Lillian emerged through the doors. Miss Lillian joined the mothers at their table while the deacons retreated to a table in the rear. As the other attendees made their way into the conference room, the instructor arrived. Their teacher was a young Asian woman in her early thirties. She gazed out across the filled-to-capacity room and seemed to notice that she was probably the youngest person in the room.

"Good morning, class. My name is Geraldine Chang, and I am an ordained minister from Kansas City, Missouri. I have advanced degrees in religion, communication, sociology, and psychology. Today's class will focus on communicating with our brothers and sisters in Christ. We will discuss how to avoid and settle conflict in a Christian manner. I have a bowl coming around, and if you have an issue you would like for me to take a stab at, please jot it down on the blank index card on your table and place it in the bowl. You will remain anonymous. Let's begin by watching this short movie."

The video showed skits of people interacting in the church. It showed an usher making contact with two members. Each member asked the usher the same question, but the usher's reaction in both scenarios was perceived differently because of the usher's posture and demeanor. The next skit showed the deacons interacting with the congregation. Two deacons asked the congregation the same question. The congregation's reaction was very different because of the tone presented by each deacon.

"Okay, class," Ms. Chang said, "by now you should have gotten the gist of what we are hoping to accomplish with this class. Let's analyze the skit we saw with the deacons. Both deacons asked the congregation to lead a hymn. Why were the congregation's responses so different?"

Mother Janie raised her hand and then stood when the instructor motioned for her to do so. "From what I observed, the first deacon had a frown on his face, and he wasn't asking—he was demanding the congregation to lead a hymn. That was the wrong way. He came across as argumentative and hostile. My momma always said you can catch more flies with honey than vinegar."

As the class laughed and applauded, Ms. Chang told Mother Janie, "Your analogy is perfect, and you are correct in your assessment of the situation. Great job! Now, Mother Janie, have you ever encountered anything like this at your church?"

Without hesitation Mother Janie blurted out, "We have, and it has impacted how our deacons are perceived. At one time the deacons were perceived as solid rocks, caretakers, and protectors; now they are perceived as obstacles, and sometimes as evildoers."

Deacon Evans raised his hand. Ms. Chang called on him, so he stood and said, "Ms. Chang, the men sitting with me at this table are the deacons at the church that Mother Janie and the occupants of her table belong to, and we can't sit idle while she says those bad things about us."

Loving this dialogue, Ms. Chang encouraged Deacon Evans to explain why this sharing of feelings and information was making him uncomfortable.

"Well, we the deacons are blamed for everything. When the snow hasn't been shoveled, we are to blame. When the church is too cold or hot, we are blamed. When the church can't loan members money, we the deacons are accused of being stingy with the church's money. When a pastor quits or abandons his position, the deacons ran him off. When members move their membership, the deacons are again blamed. I am not saying we are blameless in everything, but we don't control everything in the church. Also, we like to be acknowledged when we are doing a good job."

Mother Janie jumped back into the discussion: "Now, Deacon Evans, let me be sure I understand what you are saying. You feel we need to praise the deacons when they do a good job because this will encourage you all to do a better job at all other times?"

Ms. Chang could only smile. She admired Mother Janie for correctly using the "restate technique" covered in the film they had just watched.

Feeling as if a breakthrough was forthcoming, Deacon Evans grinned and said, "You are close, Mother Janie."

"Okay, then you and the deacons must focus on doing a better job so that we can start patting you on the back, because as it stands right now, we haven't seen any actions performed by the deacons worthy of praise or a pat on the back—aside from Deacon King's faithful service as our van driver."

Deacon Evans scowled at her, then, with his arms folded over his chest, he looked at Ms. Chang and said, "See what I am talking about? This is the drama we are dealing with on a daily basis at our church." He pointed toward the mothers. "Those women are hard to please. They have brainwashed the entire congregation against the deacons. Many Sundays we stand before the congregation looking stupid."

"Well," Mother Janie said, "maybe if you would learn the words to the songs you are singing or put your glasses on when reading the scriptures, you could eliminate the stupid-looking problem."

Ms. Chang gently and calmly asked, "Deacon Evans, do you honestly believe these sweet, angelic mothers would attempt to brainwash the very congregation of the church they so dearly love? Remember, denial and jealousy are very ugly in the church. Confession is good for the soul."

Smiling and looking even more saintly, the mothers nodded.

Deacon Evans threw his hands up in the air and shouted, "They are doing it again!"

As he took his seat, the other deacons at the table shifted their chairs a few feet away from him.

Ms. Chang waded back in. "Deacon Evans, I want you to know that there is help for you and your deacons. As a deacon, you must lead by example. You must remember your oath as a deacon and remember that God does not want confusion and turmoil in the church. Further, you should not be looking for a pat on the back from the congregation, for your reward is in heaven. Please remember the scriptures; I believe the ones coming to mind for you are in the book of James. Let's start with James 3:13–18." She opened her Bible. "Verse 13 reads, 'Who is a wise man and endued with knowledge among you? let him shew out of a good conversation his works with meekness of wisdom.' Then verse 14 reads: 'But if ye have bitter envying and strife in your hearts, glory not, and lie not against the truth.'"

Mother Kellie could be heard in the background, saying, "Lies, lies, and lies … something Deacon Evans is all too familiar with."

The leader continued. "Verse 15 reads: 'This wisdom descendeth not from above, but is earthly, sensual, devilish.'"

Now a few mothers shouted, "Amen!"

"Verse 16 reads: 'For where envying and strife is, there is confusion and every evil work.' Verse 17 reads, 'But the wisdom that is from above is first pure, then peaceable, gentle, and easy to be intreated, full of mercy and good fruits, without partiality, and without hypocrisy.' Lastly, verse 18 reads, 'And the fruit of righteousness is sown in peace of them that make peace.'

"One other verse I would like to read for you, Deacon Evans, is James 3, verses 8 and 10; they are as follows: 'But the tongue can no man tame, it is an unruly evil, full of deadly poison.'" As Ms. Chang

LASHAUNDA K. JACKSON-WILLIAMS

faced Deacon Evans, she asked, "Does this sound familiar to you?" She smiled. "Of course it does. Let me continue on because this next verse is really going to sound familiar to you." Ms. Chang's eyes lit up as she asked Deacon Evans, "Ready for this one? This is going to blow you away, Deacon Evans. Verse 10 reads, 'Out of the same mouth proceedeth blessing and cursing. My brethren, these things ought not so to be.'"

"No they shouldn't!" Miss Lillian shouted.

The mothers gasped and smiled at Miss Lillian's boldness.

"Deacon Evans," Ms. Chang said, "the Lord not only asked me to share these scriptures with you, but he also wanted me to pray for you. We are going to arm you with the scriptures you need to change from your evil ways before you leave this training."

A distraught and embarrassed Deacon Evans looked drained as the entire class applauded.

Ms. Chang then shouted, "Mothers, the Lord has heard your pleas and cries, and is speaking to me! Today we are going to have a breakthrough and stomp the devil out of Deacon Evans. Are you with me, Mothers! How about you, class?"

The mothers and Miss Lillian stood on their feet, praising the Lord, and the rest of the class followed suit. Deacon Evans jerked back after he felt Deacon Carter nudging him to go up front. His reluctance caused Ms. Chang to come to his table and grab his arm. Deacon Evans trudged up front with her. One of the big burly men sitting at the table across from the mothers offered his chair in the middle of the room for Deacon Evans.

As Deacon Evans made it up front to the chair, he felt overcome with grief and began to weep. Miss Lillian walked over to Deacon Evans, offered him a handful of tissues, smiled at him, and took her seat. Ms. Chang slapped her Bible down on his head and proceeded to start praying for him. "Please, Lord, intervene and heal Deacon Evans, his family, his deacons. Show him how to not only be a better man, but a better deacon. Lord, work on his tongue. Lord, remove the bitterness, nastiness, jealousy, evil, and hostility he has toward these sweet and blessed mothers. Lord, surround him with angels so that he won't be tempted to use profane and bad language. Keep him in your care."

Then Ms. Chang shouted, "Devil, you release this man!" She grabbed her Bible with both hands as she gritted her teeth and smacked Deacon Evans in the forehead, which caused him to weep. The deacons back at his table laughed. She then placed her Bible on a nearby table and grabbed her holy oil. As she slapped oil all over Deacon Evans' face, Ms. Chang shouted, "Devil! You release Deacon Evans' tongue and mind. Get out of his head and mind! Right now, we are going to stomp you out. Now, class, come gather around Deacon Evans as we stomp the devil out of him. Come on, class."

As the class moved forward and formed a circle around Deacon Evans, he dropped his head in his lap and continued to sob.

Finally Ms. Chang nodded. "Class, take your seats. I think Deacon Evans has been set free. Mothers and deacons, reclaim your brother."

The mothers rallied around Deacon Evans, hugging and kissing him. Miss Lillian, though, had remained seated the whole time. She just couldn't find it in herself to believe that Deacon Evans had been changed. As the mothers and deacons took their seats, Deacon Evans shook Ms. Chang's hand and thanked her before he returned to his seat.

Ms. Chang shouted, "Deacon Evans, it's not over; it's just about to get started! The devil knows he has lost you, but you must continue fighting. I know these God-fearing mothers will chastise you and bring you back into the fold when they see you stepping off God's path, and if that doesn't work, the mothers can call me, and I will gladly hop a plane to come fight the devil. I am not afraid and will travel the world for my Lord and Savior."

When the class was adjourned, Mother Kellie made her way to Deacon Evans and said, "I believe what I saw today, and I am willing to forgive you as you move on to the Lord's side. I love you, Deacon Evans."

The usual grumpy expression Deacon Evans wore had changed to a gentle and confident look as he thanked Mother Kellie and promised to do better by One Way.

After he got to his cabin, Deacon Evans thought, *Mother Kellie got a lot of nerve assuming I was never on the Lord's side.*

At dinner that night, the mothers couldn't stop chatting about Miss Chang and Deacon Evans. They laughed all evening. Mother Mille said, "That man should definitely be scared of the Word now, as many times as he got slapped upside his head with that thick leather Bible."

The next morning as Miss Lillian, the mothers, and deacons exited the cruise ship, Mother Mae told everyone, "We sent for a big limousine again so that we may all ride together back to the airport. Deacons, will you join us?"

A jubilant Deacon Evans answered, "Yes, ma'am, we will."

Soon enough laughter erupted from the limousine when Mother Millie's wig got caught up in the moon roof as she was climbing in.

"This $200 wig is definitely going back to One Way, Ohio, with me," Mother Millie said. "Do I have it on straight, Mother Addie?"

"No, honey," she said, pulling the wig off and readjusting it to the front. "Now that looks better." Mother Addie smiled, looking into Mother Millie's eyes.

"Thank you, Mother."

"I don't know about anybody else, but my soul is sure on fire from this wonderful cruise," Mother Mae said as she wiped sweat from her brow and allowed the air-conditioning to cool her down.

Wearing an enticing nightgown, Lulabelle waited in the living room for her husband to return home from five days in the Caribbean, getting empowered—and hopefully getting even—with the mothers. Lulabelle was anxious to hear about what the deacons were able to uncover that would bring shame on the mothers. She kept floating the thought of their gambling, dancing, picking up men, and drinking. She finally heard her husband opening and then closing the garage door shortly after midnight, and she hurried toward the kitchen to greet him. He had already made it into the kitchen, where he'd dropped his luggage and grabbed a pitcher of lemonade from the refrigerator.

"Lulabelle, are you awake?" he called out. "I got something to tell you if you are."

Lulabelle came around the corner into the kitchen and dropped the robe to reveal her naughty nightgown.

Deacon Evans embraced her in a hug as he whispered, "I sure missed you. You are not going to believe what happened on the cruise."

With a smile and an inquisitive look on her face, Lulabelle took a guess: "I know it has something to do with those meddling mothers. Were they gambling and drinking the whole time?"

"No, no, baby, it's about me."

Now Lulabelle eyed him. "You better just tell me because I am running out of guesses right now."

"Lu, I was overcome by the Holy Spirit and the Lord broke me down. I am a changed man."

"Say what?" Lulabelle hurried to put her robe back on before she tilted her head and then leaned in close to sniff her husband for the smell of alcohol. "Of course you are filled with the Holy Spirit; I wouldn't marry a man that wasn't filled with the Holy Spirit."

Deacon Evans smiled at Lulabelle, touched her hand, and said calmly, "Baby, you are not ready for this, but I know the Lord is working on me. I have never felt so much remorse and relief until after the intervention by one of the seminar instructors, the mothers, and the deacons."

Lulabelle paused. Something in his voice unsettled her. Her face flushed as her voice began to rise. "Deacon Harold Evans, you let those heathens and those pathetic deacons convince you that you were the problem. I can't believe you fell for that. Think about it! You know what, I am going to bed and don't want to hear anything else about this."

A joyous Harold told Lulabelle, "Sweet dreams," and then he sang all the way into the family room, where he watched the I Love Jesus Channel until he fell asleep.

MINGLING WITH THE SINGLE FOLK

The Single Folk Ministry, formed under Pastor Walker's leadership, was a group of thirty-eight single One Way members, ranging in age from twenty-three to seventy-three. The ministry provided support to single members who shared similar spiritual, relational, personal, and financial issues. What was unique about the group was that Pastor Walker, a divorced and single man, was very familiar with the challenges faced by single people at One Way. Under his leadership, the group had grown to more than a hundred members.

Some members expressed a desire to continue meeting after Pastor Walker's abrupt departure. Since Deacon Evans had always felt that a married and successful person should lead this ministry, he had jumped at the opportunity to take it over. He never understood how a single or divorced person could inspire someone to get married if they never had been married or had failed at it. Many members weren't exactly thrilled about Deacon Evans filling in, but they accepted it so that their ministry could resume. For others, it was a way to peek inside the seemingly perfect marriage of Deacon and Sister Evans.

Brother Leon Love was an engineer at the local utility company, and he was also known as the church Casanova because he had never refused any woman from One Way who had shamed herself by throwing herself at him. He'd kindly offered to host the first meeting under Deacon Evans' leadership at his home.

The One Way Church rumor mill reported that Leon had bedded more than half of the female members of the Single Folk Ministry, including Miss Lillian and Mother Addie. Deacon Evans obliged to lead the meeting, but made it clear to Leon from the start that he did not want any foolishness. Leon told Deacon Evans that he didn't know what he had heard, but assured Deacon Evans that he was a young man on fire for the Lord and would do everything in his power to support Deacon Evans as he temporarily took over the Single Folk Ministry.

Brother Love made sure meeting announcements were mailed, e-mailed, read during church announcements, and posted on the church's bulletin board.

As Deacon Evans was preparing for the Single Folk Ministry meeting, Lulabelle asked him why he was wasting valuable time fooling with losers. "This makes absolutely no sense to me. Tell me why," she said.

"Sure, I know this ministry is full of rejects, scorned lovers, unattractive folks, and mentally unstable folk that need help, but they need to hear from someone in a position of authority at the church that they admire, like you and me. We have a good solid marriage, and we are a beautiful and happy couple. What they really want to know is how we do it and keep doing it. Lu, they are struggling to get what we got. It would be a sin for us not to share our solid marriage with these lonely and desperate single folks."

Lulabelle chuckled and said, "Hmm, I'll be going with you tonight to keep an eye on the single women who just may be looking for a sugar daddy. Just don't let these single misfits fall in love with each other," Lulabelle snapped. "And if it is suggested that you host one of these lonely single meetings at our house, please politely decline."

After she said that, Deacon Evans raised his eyebrow, and she responded with a trace of a smile. They both laughed as they continued to get ready.

Brother Love's bachelor pad was way on the north side of town—not the part of town where someone would just happen be in the neighborhood. It was a brick ranch home with four bedrooms, two bathrooms, a formal living room and dining room, a family room, and a huge eat-in kitchen. The so-called House of Love boasted a large front yard with a circular driveway. One couldn't help but notice the lush landscaping surrounding the home. In the backyard stood a huge privacy fence that concealed his hot tub and workout equipment from neighbors.

Leon's six-figure job and elegant taste afforded him the ability to drive a brand new, jet-black BMW that made the women at One Way lovesick. Because Leon was single and without children, he had been deemed as filet mignon at the church. Leon did not stand too tall, but his hazel eyes and curly hair bamboozled women at One Way. Mother Janie described him as a young Smokey Robinson who couldn't carry a tune. Mother Millie didn't fool with him because one winter Sunday when he was helping her up the steps of the church, he let her slip and fall down the steps while he took a peek at Millicent Baker's hefty behind. Once Mother Millie got up and into the church safely, thanks to Deacon King, she scolded Leon something fierce.

Miss Lillian, Mother Janie, and Sister Bessie Davis were the first to arrive at Leon's home, as they were all members of the Single Folk Ministry and in charge of the food. As Leon opened the door, he flashed a lucky grin, licked his lips, and said, "Welcome to the House of Love."

Bessie and Miss Lillian blushed and giggling, but Mother Janie elbowed her way between Bessie and Miss Lillian and shouted, "Leon, don't just stand there! You see us with these boxes. Stop licking your lips and grab some boxes."

"M-My bad," Leon said. "Let me help you lovely ladies." As Leon grabbed the boxes, he apologized to Mother Janie and then he led them into his home.

When they stepped into Leon's home, Mother Janie got very quiet and said, "Leon, you have done well for yourself. What a nice place. Now where is the kitchen?"

Leon led the ladies to the left as he carried the boxes of food.

After they entered his huge kitchen, Mother Janie said, "Baby, how do I work this fancy microwave?"

Leon showed Mother Janie how to work the microwave and the stove. He then told them that he had stored beverages for the meeting in the refrigerator. On the counter were serving plates, paper plates, paper cups, napkins, and utensils. Leon then disappeared into the living room to straighten up—and take another glance at himself in the mirror by the front door.

While he was in the living room practicing poses and checking himself out, the ladies began searching the cupboards and refrigerator. Bessie found wine everywhere. She commented to Miss Lillian and Mother Janie, "Leon sure does a lot of drinking." Just as Mother Janie opened the refrigerator, she shouted, "Mercy!" Right in her face were two twelve packs and a twenty-four-count box of beer.

Mother Janie wiped her brow and said, "No wonder Leon was licking his lips with all this beer in here. He is hoping to get lucky tonight! He ought to be ashamed of all this devil juice. He must have this party confused with another because I don't see beverages in here that are suitable for the Single Folk Ministry."

Mother Janie signaled for Bessie to come take a look in the refrigerator. She winked at Bessie and they both shook their heads. Miss Lillian, though, began to unpack the food to get things organized. She was smitten with Leon and his pad. When Miss Lillian opened Leon's cupboard, she saw wine and whiskey. She commented to Mother Janie and Bessie, "I don't see anything wrong with a little beer, wine, and whiskey. Leon doesn't seem to be a man who can't hold his liquor. I find him rather intriguing."

Bessie whispered to Mother Janie, "And you call *me* delirious and man-hungry."

The doorbell rang almost continuously for the next twenty minutes as members began to arrive. Deacon King had come along with twelve members whom he'd transported in the church van. As Deacon Evans and Lulabelle arrived, Leon greeted them. Deacon

Evans showed up wearing dark jeans, a burgundy turtleneck, and a blazer. Dressed in such casual attire, Deacon Evans appeared calm as he immediately began to work the crowd. Lulabelle also appeared relaxed and at ease, dressed in jeans and a sleeveless sweater. After helping Lulabelle remove her jacket, Leon winked, licked his lips, and said, "Welcome, Mrs. Evans to the House of Love. Please make yourself at home."

Lulabelle blushed even as she noticed his fine taste in art and furniture. Leon winked again at Lulabelle as he left the room to go hang up her jacket.

Deacon Evans got distracted as he greeted and chatted away with members already seated. Eve Dixon, Isabel Jones, JR Cloud, Ginny Dexter, and Paula Taylor all giggled at each other as they watched Lulabelle's behavior around Leon. Her mannerisms were so unlike the big, bad front that Lulabelle put on at church that it took them by surprise. Meanwhile Deacon Evans popped his head into the kitchen to greet Mother Janie and Bessie. He asked them whether they needed any help, and they both gave him a loud "NO!" This drew laughter from all three of them. Before Deacon Evans departed the kitchen, he commented on how good the food smelled and that he could hardly wait to eat.

Mother Janie, Miss Lillian, and Bessie began bringing the food from the kitchen to the family room. Leon had set up a table in front of a huge bay window. The bay window showcased his lovely manicured backyard. Leon built a nice cozy fire on the opposite side of the family room where all had assembled. All the while, Lulabelle couldn't take her eyes off Leon and his exquisite home furnishings.

As Miss Lillian was attempting to get Leon's attention while serving coffee, she accidentally spilled some on Deacon Evans' sport coat. Miss Lillian apologized, and Deacon Evans told her not to worry as he jumped up to prevent the spill from spreading to his pants. He asked Leon where the bathroom was located, and Leon pointed down the hall. After Deacon Evans cleaned up and returned, Miss Lillian went on again, expressing how sorry she was about the accident. Deacon

Evans again told her not to worry about it. Miss Lillian turned to Lulabelle and said, "I can't believe I was so clumsy. I really didn't mean to do it. Gosh, I don't remember ever having an accident like that."

Lulabelle said, "I think Deacon Evans has made it clear that he understands this was an unfortunate accident. We really don't care to hear any more of your rambling about it, okay, Miss Lillian?"

Miss Lillian nodded her head. "You are right, I've said enough," she said, and then returned to the kitchen to assist the serving crew.

Mother Janie and Bessie announced that the food setup was complete. Deacon Evans asked everyone to gather around and hold hands as he offered prayer for the food. Deacon Evans grabbed Lulabelle's right hand with his rough, calloused hands; and Leon grabbed Lulabelle's left hand with his soft and strong hands. As Deacon Evans began to pray, Leon began squeezing, massaging, and rubbing Lulabelle's hand. It sent Lulabelle into an erotic frenzy. As she began moaning with her eyes closed and a sensual smile across her face, her husband continued blessing the food. Eve, Ginny, and Isabel were doing their best to stifle their laughter. Deacon Evans thought his wife was caught up in the Spirit, as did Mother Janie, so Deacon Evans kept going with the prayer. As Leon continued massaging and stroking the palm of Lulabelle's hand, Lulabelle worked up a sweat and she took to hollering along with moaning. Her hollering and moaning made Mother Janie holler even louder, which encouraged Deacon Evans to keep going. Finally Deacon King, who could not take his eyes off the food, gave a friendly shout, "Gone and bless this food, Deacon Evans." This brought Deacon Evans back to the matter at hand and he ended his prayer. Immediately after the prayer ended, Lulabelle, drenched in sweat, darted down the hall to the bathroom. Leon smiled as he watched her make her way down the hall. Eve, Ginny, and Isabel couldn't control their laughter any longer and told Deacon Evans what a remarkable prayer he had prayed. With a proud grin on his face, Deacon Evans thanked them.

Even Mother Janie couldn't contain herself. She called on Deacon Evans and said, "Deacon Evans, I don't know what came over you, but you sure prayed tonight. I feel this meeting tonight is going to be blessed because we started out with powerful prayer."

Deacon Evans embraced Mother Janie and thanked her. As everyone was making their way through the line, Lulabelle reappeared, looking flushed. Deacon Evans looked at her and asked her if she was okay, and she told him that during his prayer, something got a hold of her and she'd lost control. Deacon Evans told her that whatever it was, it helped him too. She smiled.

After everyone got settled with their plates, Leon brought out some punch, which he announced to be "holy punch." Mother Janie gave him a look, pulled him aside, and whispered into his ear, "Leon, there better not be any unholy stuff up in this punch or your behind will be mine, you understand?"

Leon stared into Mother Janie's eyes. He saw the seriousness in her expression and quickly returned to the kitchen and dumped the punch into the sink, returning with a pitcher of lemonade.

Deacon Evans stood in front of the fireplace as he addressed the group. His topic for the evening was "Loving Yourself." The group members pulled out their Bibles when he referred them to Proverbs 17:17. As he began to read, Leon, seated next to Lulabelle, gave her a gentle nudge and a wink. Lulabelle blushed, but kept her focus on her husband. She already felt embarrassed by the entire situation and believed she was succumbing to the behavior of the women who were seated in the room.

Deacon Evans proceeded to tell the group, "If you don't love God, you can't begin to love yourself, and if you don't love God and yourself, ain't no way you going to be able to love anyone else. What Lulabelle and I have is true and solid love. We have never had eyes for no one else but each other. We both love God, we both love ourselves, and we love each other, ain't that right, Lulabelle?"

Staring down at her Bible, Lulabelle was still trying to figure out what had happened during prayer and hadn't heard a word her husband had said. She jumped when Deacon Evans called her name a second time. She responded with a weak "Yes, Deacon Evans?" Not even sure what she had just said, Deacon Evans smiled and winked at her, and she nodded in agreement.

As Deacon Evans began fielding questions from the group, he received a question from Leon: "Deacon Evans, how do you keep Lulabelle loving you year after year?"

With her mouth half-open, Lulabelle gave Leon a "How dare you" look. Deacon Evans jumped right in and said, "I hold her hand," which drew laughter from the group. He then proceeded to say that she was "easy," which immediately popped Leon's eyes wide open, but Deacon Evans quickly said, "She is easy to love because she is strong, giving, gentle, patient, and loves me back the way I love her. I might send her to a day spa for her birthday and shower her with clothes and jewelry. I remember the small things and the big things. I show her every day that I love her. Eventually those days turn into weeks, to months, and to years."

Leon then told Deacon Evans that he hoped to find a woman just like Lulabelle once he learned to love God and himself.

Mother Janie, who was hip to Leon's game, gave Leon a frown as she shook her head at him in disgust. Miss Lillian, though, was eating it up. She kept smiling and grinning at Leon, hoping he would look her way, but he couldn't take his eyes off Lulabelle.

Bessie posed the next question: "Deacon Evans, I love God and surely I love myself. Why is it taking so long for me to find a boyfriend? I surely have been looking for the last fifteen years."

Miss Lillian jumped right in and said, "I know how you feel, Bessie, because I am going through the same dry spell."

Deacon Evans looked at Bessie and responded, "Maybe you're setting your standards too high, you know? At your age, you need to be grateful for each day and every breath."

With a tear running down her face, Bessie rose from her seat and said to Deacon Evans, "Show me some respect!"

Everyone in the crowd seemed shocked by Deacon Evans' comment. To diffuse the situation, Deacon Evans called Lulabelle up front to give her take on their marriage. As Lulabelle came before the gathered crowd to speak about the high and low points of her marriage, Deacon Evans took her seat, right next to Leon. As Leon flashed Lulabelle a coy grin and licked his lips yet again, Lulabelle began to blush and giggle. Deacon Evans nodded his head when he saw Lulabelle look his way, smiling and blushing, thinking her reaction was directed at him. In order to get through the ordeal, Lulabelle knew she would have to face the ladies on her left and turn completely away from Leon and Deacon Evans.

Once she turned that way, she was able to focus. Lulabelle started out by saying, "Ladies, I was once in your shoes: lonely, desperate, searching for a man." An "Amen" came from the right corner, and as everyone turned that way, they saw Miss Lillian clapping and nodding in agreement with what Lulabelle had just said. Lulabelle continued. "Now with the Internet and singles chat sites, I know many of the ladies are still desperately searching for Mr. Right. But please listen to what I am saying. I was not sure what God had in store for me, so I started reading everything I could get my hands on about getting and keeping a man. Then I remember my grandmother telling me, 'Lulabelle, hold out. God is getting you ready for the man of your dreams.'

"When that man comes, you will know it. It will be right. It won't feel forced or out of place. You will be compatible with each other. What I found in Harold Evans was my soul mate. The very thought of him makes me smile and blush. We could be miles apart or a room apart, and I still get excited about my husband."

The majority of the group sat with their mouths wide open after Lulabelle made that comment. Mother Janie asked, "Do you mean that Deacon Evans over there?"

An agitated Lulabelle responded, "Who else would I be speaking about?"

Mother Janie looked at Lulabelle and said, "I don't know; that's why I asked."

Lulabelle dismissed Mother Janie's interruption and continued. "Harold is my best friend. Many people think I wear the pants in our marriage because I am bossy. Believe it or not, Harold got me this way. He has spoiled me beyond belief. I know he has my back. I don't want for anything, and he puts me second only to God. Ladies, know your place. A man does not want a woman he can't take home to his mother. He's not interested in your tattoos, body piercing, and other fads that will be constant reminders of times that did not include him."

Miss Lillian raised her hand. She stood as Lulabelle acknowledged her. "I have a male friend that refuses to take me out before 10:00 p.m. When we do go out, we meet during a late movie that has already started. We will sit in his car, which has heavily tinted windows, to eat a meal. He tells me repeatedly he is busy during the day with work and that he's not a morning person. I personally think he is ashamed to be seen with me. I need a man's perspective on this one. What can I do to get him to take me out during daylight hours? What should I do?"

As Miss Lillian took her seat, Deacon Evans gave an arrogant grin and said, "Pray."

After seeing the reaction of the class, Lulabelle jumped in and said, "Outside beauty will fade. Inside beauty, common sense, and book sense will take you a long way. Learn how to talk intelligently. Don't be loud in your talk or your appearance. Be yourself. When you are yourself, it's natural, it's consistent with the person God created, and the person you present to the world every day."

Lulabelle had found her stride in speaking to the crowd, and she was smiling and enjoying it. "So when God sends Mr. Right your way, you need to be ready. Always keep your hair clean and neatly groomed. I am not saying that you need to go to the beauty salon every week, but keep your hair looking nice. Hygiene is extremely important. Remember to bathe and put on deodorant. It's an awful place to be when you are standing next to a woman who is not wearing deodorant. Imagine that woman being you. After you bathe, put on clean clothes. Now, ladies and men, this is common sense. Keep clean clothes. Every woman should own a nice suit, a nice dress, a nice pair of pants, a couple of nice blouses, and a decent pair of jeans. From one woman to another woman, it is imperative that you maintain decent underwear, decent shoes, and stockings."

Miss Lillian had flipped to her fifth page of taking notes. She was jotting down everything Lulabelle had to say.

"Now I am not telling you to go out and neglect your kids by buying stuff you can't afford or charge your credit cards to the max, but add things gradually to your wardrobe. If you make a commitment to buy a dress one month, then next month buy a pair a shoes, and so on, you will be less likely to break the bank.

"You must be prepared for the unexpected. As a woman, we must wear many hats, and preparation is vital. We must always prepare for emergencies and always have a backup plan. If you want a man to respect you, you must respect yourself. If he hears you on the phone cursing out somebody to get their attention, then he will do the same to you when he needs to get your attention. Respect yourself. If you pay every time you go out, then he will continue to allow you to pay because it appears that you want to pay all the time."

Lulabelle waved her index finger and walked from one side of the room to the other as she continued. "Ladies and gentlemen, let's talk about looks. Many of us in this room are being way, way, and way too picky when it comes to looks. Many of you are tore up and looking for a Halle Berry or Denzel Washington." Lulabelle snapped her fingers twice. "Snap out of that. You are in One Way, Ohio, and you are just going to have to work with what we got in One Way. I know many of you are thinking that all of the good men, like my Harold, are gone, but not necessarily. I would rather have Harold than a good-looking broke dummy. Understand me. I can get used to ugly, but I can't get used to stupid."

The crowd gasped at what Lulabelle just said. They weren't sure whether it was okay to laugh or not, so they looked back at Deacon Evans, who no longer had a grin on his face. He stood up and said, "Lu, I will take over from here." Lulabelle thanked everyone for their attention and took her seat.

"Group," Deacon Evans said, "in summary, I believe what Lulabelle was trying to say is you only get one opportunity to make a first impression. First impressions are so important. If you are tired looking and your hair is always a mess, you will definitely not make a good first impression." Deacon Evans looked directly at Mother Janie as he made the statement, and he knew a reaction would be forthcoming.

Mother Janie looked to her right and her left and saw that Deacon Evans' eyes remained fixed on her. She raised her hand and said, "Excuse me, Deacon Evans, but don't write a check your behind can't cash."

Mother Janie's comment drew laughter from the crowd, and Deacon Evans, not to be outdone, told Mother Janie, "This is exactly why you have been a member of the singles ministry for more than fifty years. No man, anywhere, in his right mind and with good eyesight, would put up with you. You hear me. No man, anywhere, in his right mind would put up with you."

"Oh my!" Miss Lillian said. "What an awful thing to say. Have you lost your mind?" She shook her head. "I knew this was a bad idea to have you lead this meeting."

Miss Lillian looked at Mother Janie and felt the pain of the words spewing from Deacon Evans' mouth. "I make a motion that we immediately adjourn this meeting," Miss Lillian said. "May I get a second?"

Bessie rose to her feet in agreement with Miss Lillian's motion.

Miss Lillian then turned to Deacon Evans and told him, "Sir, the meeting is adjourned." Miss Lillian then went to see about Mother Janie, as did the rest of the group. As they huddled around Mother Janie, they began pointing and giving Deacon Evans evil stares. The group took his attack personally, and they couldn't believe Deacon Evans would be so insensitive to Mother Janie.

Deacon Evans made his way to the center of the room and said, "I will say when the meeting is adjourned. It is NOW adjourned!"

Leon helped Lulabelle on with her coat and whispered into her ear "Anytime you want to come back, you are welcome."

Lulabelle rushed out of Leon's family room to find Deacon Evans. During the car ride home, Deacon Evans asked Lulabelle if she'd had a good time.

Lulabelle responded, "I had a nice time. That Leon is something else. Harold, another thing, you really need to be more sensitive to these folks' feelings and stop with the Lulabelle this and Lulabelle that. I found that to be annoying, and another thing—"

Before Lulabelle could get anything else out, Deacon Evans' cell phone began to ring, and he immediately grabbed it and began talking to shut Lulabelle up.

LORD OF THE UNIVERSE

A torrential rainstorm started minutes before Sunday morning service. Guest preacher Reverend Enrique Morales was seated on the first pew, ready to deliver the morning sermon. The deacons were already fifteen minutes into morning devotions when Sister Melody Note rushed through the vestibule doors, strutting up front to the piano. Melody, as always, disregarded the ushers as they asked her to wait until prayer or scripture was finished before she moved about within the sanctuary. As usual, she had everyone's undivided attention. Melody had been married five times and was engaged again. This time she was engaged to Reverend Enrique Morales, a Latino gentleman she'd met on the Internet, and who had moved from Miami, Florida, to One Way, Ohio. He was definitely good looking, but spoke very little English. Many members thought he was merely eye candy, used by Melody to get under the skin of all the jealous women at One Way, as well as the skin of her former husbands and beaus.

Melody's position had always been, "I need a man." This position had taken Melody down many long, dark roads. Her mother, Mother Suzie, had no explanation for Melody's behavior. She simply told people Melody was just crazy, but Lord knows the child could play the piano, organ, guitar, and violin. Mother Suzie previously lived with

Melody. After witnessing the revolving door of men in and out of her daughter's home, she had to get her own place.

When Reverend Morales began his sermon, Deacon Evans, sitting on the front pew, set the timer on his watch. As Reverend Morales opened his Bible and then his mouth, the congregation was in shock. Reverend Morales' entire sermon was in Spanish. The man spoke only a few words of broken English. Mother Mae whispered to Mother Janie, "I thought Deacon Evans was investigating the background of the ministers he would have as guest speakers."

Mother Janie told Mother Mae she'd heard Deacon Evans didn't have time, and he was relying on the committee to present names to the deacons for prior approval. Apparently this one slipped through the cracks. They both giggled and nodded in agreement with Reverend Morales.

There were a few people in the sanctuary who actually understood Spanish and knew what Reverend Morales was saying. Melody, for one, knew Spanish, and fully comprehended what he was saying, and she supported her man by shouting in Spanish. As the rain outside intensified into thunder and lightning, Reverend Morales took his sermon up another notch. He held his Bible up in the air and fell to his knees with tears streaming down his face. As Melody made her way to the organ, Reverend Morales began to sing "Amazing Grace" in English.

Mother Addie grabbed Mother Janie's arm and said, "I don't know what he was saying but Jesus is taking over. I feel the Spirit, Janie, how about you? Child, that man is preaching. Those tears and sweat, it can't be nothing but Jesus."

The entire congregation stood in amazement and shouted encouragement to Reverend Morales. He knew all the verses of the hymn. After he sang, five souls came to Christ and requested membership in One Way. Reverend Morales himself and Deacon King's grandchildren joined the church and requested to be baptized. It was a glorious day at One Way.

Miss Lillian then briefly met with each new member and completed a mini church membership application. She completed Reverend Morales' application first, with the help of Melody Note, and then proceeded to Deacon King and his grandchildren.

Deacon King was prepared. He knew Miss Lillian wasn't fond of him and wanted to expedite this encounter to avoid the need for a follow-up discussion. He provided copies of each of his grandchildren's birth certificates and completed all three membership applications. Miss Lillian avoided looking into his eyes, and spoke while staring at Deacon King's tie.

Miss Lillian then made a snide comment to Deacon King about the whereabouts of the children's grandmother. Deacon King told her point blank, "It's none of your business. None at all."

Miss Lillian took off her glasses and told Deacon King, "Look, I've been very patient with you. Answer my question, okay?"

Deacon King took the high road. He grabbed his grandchildren and walked away from Miss Lillian.

She shouted, "I am so tired of people in this church disregarding me and my feelings. My parents, grandparents, and great-grandparents built this church to be what it is today!" Shaking her head side to side, she continued. "I can't take this anymore. I can't do this. I am done."

The few members left in the sanctuary exchanged dubious glances at Miss Lillian and rushed to the exit as they were unsure what her next move might be. Miss Lillian barged through the vestibule, talking to herself and shoving folks and children to get outside in the rain. She climbed into her white Cadillac and maneuvered it to block the church van, the mothers' van, and Deacon and Lulabelle Evans' car from leaving. Many of the members peered out the church's main entrance doors, watching the situation unfold. They saw the big Cadillac blocking the path of the vans that were parked one behind the other in one row, while in the next row was Deacon Evans' car, which had three cars parked behind him.

Inside the van already occupied by the Mothers' Board and driven by Deacon King, everyone figured Miss Lillian had run out of gas—until Deacon King told them about her strange behavior in the church.

Mother Janie said, "I would hate to see Miss Lillian get whipped out here in the rain over some foolishness."

"Amen," said a few of the mothers and Deacon King.

From inside Deacon and Sister Evans' vehicle, they felt Miss Lillian's car tap their front fender, and they were trying to tell her to move, with horn blowing and hand motions. With the rain pouring down, they figured she was having trouble navigating her Cadillac, as it was an old and very long vehicle. Because Miss Lillian was a short woman, this made perfect sense. Deacon Evans blew his horn again, and Miss Lillian turned and looked in the opposite direction. This infuriated Deacon Evans, since he and Lulabelle now had a very clear view of Miss Lillian and believed she was having one of her tantrums.

Everyone watched Deacon Evans emerge from his vehicle and run to the driver's side of Miss Lillian's car, which was parked at the hood of his car. He knocked on the window to get Miss Lillian's attention. Miss Lillian looked at him, partially lowered her window, and asked Deacon Evans with a wide grin on her face, "How can I help you, Deacon?"

Deacon Evans looked at her and shouted, "Move this train out of the way! You are blocking everyone in!"

Miss Lillian then lowered her window completely, waved her finger at Deacon Evans, and shouted, "I am having a real problem with your attitude!" She then turned her car off, scooted to the passenger side of her car, got out, and began walking home in the rain. No umbrella, no coat. She proudly carried her purse on her shoulder and her Bible in her arms and walked up One Way Lane without looking back.

The members couldn't believe Miss Lillian's behavior. As the occupants of the blocked vehicles returned to the church, Deacons

Evans, King, and Carter got together and decided to call the police. The police arrived quickly, took a report, and called a tow truck to remove Miss Lillian's car. The deacons requested that the car be towed to Miss Lillian's house and that the church would deduct the cost from Miss Lillian's salary. Since the tow truck would take thirty minutes to arrive, the deacons consulted with the mothers to discuss their concerns. Deacon Evans knew his hot temper would cause him to say something inappropriate to Miss Lillian and wanted the mothers' buy-in on how to deal with this bizarre incident. The deacons wanted to fire Miss Lillian and place a restraining order against her from returning to the church. The mothers felt that was too harsh under the sketchy circumstances. The mothers requested time to speak with Miss Lillian to sort out this nightmare. The deacons agreed to allow the mothers time to speak with Miss Lillian, but they requested that if their talk didn't take place before next Sunday, they would call Miss Lillian on Saturday, asking her not to return to One Way until she had spoken with the Mothers' Board. The mothers concurred with this decision.

After the deacons left, Mother Kellie told the mothers that Miss Lillian had recently confided in her that she was struggling with menopause. Mother Janie said, "Well, I remember her telling me she was struggling with menopause back in the '80s. I think Miss Lillian is bipolar, and it certainly doesn't help that she is a Gemini."

Mother Millie told the ladies she recalled Miss Lillian's mother was a bit crazy—they'd sent her to the state hospital for six months after Miss Lillian was born. She wasn't sure if it was Miss Lillian's birth or the stint up at the state mental hospital, but when she returned, she was never the same. Mother Mae told the mothers she also recalled Miss Lillian's mother being institutionalized in the state mental hospital.

Mother Janie said to the mothers, "We need to go see Miss Lillian. Let's do it unannounced in the morning. We can't give her any opportunity to plan anything. Mother Kellie, since she and Deacon King aren't getting along, will you drive us?"

"I sure will. Let's try to get there at 8:30 a.m."

Just then, Deacon King knocked on the Mothers' Room door and announced, "The tow truck has removed Miss Lillian's car, and we can now leave, Mothers."

Some of the mothers belted out "Thank goodness" as they grabbed their raincoats and scarves and headed outside to the van. Deacon King wasn't even three blocks from the church when he peered into his rearview mirror and found the mothers fast asleep.

STRANGE BEHAVIOR

During the ride to Miss Lillian's home the next morning, the mothers speculated about what kind of mood they would find her in. As the mothers prepared to climb out of the van, they gathered their food items, bags, and purses. Mother Janie and Mother Millie made sure their Taser guns were reachable in their purses in the event that Miss Lillian got out of control.

Mother Karen said, "All I could find were my late husband's brass knuckles."

Mother Mae told the mothers that Miss Lillian would be fine; since they were bringing food, she would be receptive to their visit. "We will talk to her as if we were talking to one of our children."

Mother Millie shouted, "Then you certainly don't want me to do the talking since I shot both of my hard-headed children! That back-talking and coming in when you feel like it didn't sit well with me. You feel me, Mothers?" She looked around. "And, Mother Mae, I thought we made it clear to Mother Karen this would a weapon-free organization and our van was a weapon-free zone?"

"How can it be weapon-free when you are packing a Taser gun?"

"I see your point," Mother Millie said.

"That's right, honey: you sit and back us up as we do the talking," Mother Kellie said, then whispered to Mother Janie, "Please make sure Mother Millie isn't packing no heat in that big purse of hers."

"Child, you know I have already taken care of Millie."

The mothers said a word of prayer before departing from the van. They gripped each other's hands tightly, as they knew the mission before them was going to be difficult.

Through the large picture window on the porch, they could see the living room cluttered with visions of what looked like the early 1970s—complete with hanging macramé plant holders and a tall wicker basket with feathers sticking out here and there. They also noticed Miss Lillian sitting peacefully in her rocking chair, watching television.

When Miss Lillian heard the doorbell, she rushed to the front door and saw all of the mothers through the peephole. Wearing a T-shirt that had a picture of her deceased parents on it, Miss Lillian opened the door.

"Oh how nice!" Miss Lillian said. "Look who's come to visit. I haven't had company in years. Everyone, come on in!"

The mothers, one by one, entered carrying a covered dish, pot, or bag. The mothers stopped in their tracks as they entered the dining room. They scanned the room and noted the dark and dingy environment. Mother Mae reached to open the curtains in the dining room, and dust blew everywhere. Dead spiders were hanging in the window, but Mother Mae continued opening the curtains to allow the sunshine to flow in. Mother Millie followed Mother Mae's lead and opened the curtains on the other side of the dining room. She not only discovered dust bunnies everywhere, but mouse droppings on the windowsill. Mother Millie stood frozen in fear, but Mother Janie and Mother Kellie quickly pulled Mother Millie back away from the window. As the mothers looked to set the table, the existing tablecloth was dusty and smelled of mothballs. Mother Mae opened her bag, pulled out a disposable tablecloth, and placed it on top of the existing tablecloth. She also placed her hand sanitizer on the table.

Miss Lillian went into the kitchen to get some glasses and plates while the mothers gathered around the family photos she had displayed on the buffet in the dining room. Miss Lillian emerged from the kitchen, coming into the dining room with glasses, plates, silver-ware, and napkins.

"Thank you so much for stopping by to share breakfast with me," Miss Lillian said.

Then she sat at the head of the table as the mothers gathered in the surrounding chairs. During the breakfast conversation, Miss Lillian told the story of how her parents lent One Way the money to build the building that was now One Way. It was on the tip of Mother Mae's tongue to tell her that the church had never accepted money from her parents, but instead took out a loan at the local bank, but she held back.

Throughout the meal Mother Kellie thought she was kicking at Mother Mae's foot and kept apologizing. Finally Mother Mae asked, "Child, what are you talking about? You haven't kicked me."

Mother Kellie's voice, choked with fear, said, "I keep kicking at something."

Each of the mothers scooted their chairs back from the table and took a peek below.

"What in the world?" Mother Mae said.

All of the mothers felt a surprised upon seeing the many pairs of old shoes and boots parked in front of each chair.

Miss Lillian told the mothers that she collected shoes from deceased relatives who had eaten at her table, and she kept those shoes and boots at the table in memory of the festive occasions shared by her family in her home. The mothers all felt a stab of fear and anxiety within, but kept their faces steady. Wanting to change the subject, Mother Addie commented on how good the food tasted, her voice trembling a bit as she did so. The other mothers echoed her comments, also with shaky voices. Then the mothers remained quiet as they listened to Miss Lillian go right back to talking about her family.

Finally, tired of hearing the same sad lies about Miss Lillian's family, Mother Janie pushed back her chair and said, "Miss Lillian, I am so full. Do you mind if I start to clear the table?"

"No, not at all, Mother Janie," replied Miss Lillian as she finished her plate so that she could help Mother Janie.

The other mothers joined Mother Janie and Miss Lillian with clearing and cleaning the table, then they went to town on getting that dining room and kitchen in order. Since Miss Lillian was slow and long-winded, the mothers cleaned circles around her. During their cleaning Mothers Addie and Janie kept their eyes open for diet strawberry soda or anything else that might tie Miss Lillian to Pastor Walker's disappearance.

Before Miss Lillian knew it, she was able to see counter space and windowsills she hadn't seen in years. Exhausted after deep-cleaning Miss Lillian's kitchen and dining room, the mothers retreated into the living room. As they gazed around the room, the mothers sat motionless and speechless. The room seemed haunting, with shaggy orange carpet, a velvet portrait of black Jesus on the wall behind the sofa, and another velvet portrait of The Last Supper over the mantle place. There were the peacock feathers in the corner wicker basket, plastic covers on the furniture, ashtrays everywhere, a thirteen-inch television on top of a floor model television with a huge antenna on top of the TV, and pictures everywhere. Now the mothers really understood what Deacon King had told them years ago about when he'd dated Miss Lillian.

Mother Addie pushed aside a pair of men's slippers on the floor in front of her as she tried to get comfortable. Mother Millie held on tight to Mother Kellie's hand as she tried to keep from panicking about the two wigs and wig stands seated next to her on an end table: Miss Lillian had drawn eyes and lips on each mannequin. Someone would have thought they were in a museum, the way they were observing the contents of the living room. Mother Karen, just returning from the bathroom, whispered to the mothers, "If you think this is something, wait till you see the bathroom."

As soon as Mother Karen sat down, she began sliding off the plastic-covered chair. Finally she took her sweater off, placed it on the chair, and sat on it to prevent her from sliding again. Miss Lillian soon appeared, pushing in a dining room chair so that she could chat with the mothers, since Mother Mae had found comfort in her favorite rocking chair. As Mother Karen readjusted herself into the chair, she told Miss Lillian how nice she had kept the house and how proud her parents would be of her. The other mothers nervously nodded and smiled in agreement, unsure of how Miss Lillian would take the compliment. Miss Lillian, with a bold smile on her face, thanked the mothers and told them she had really been working hard over the years on keeping the house up to her mother's immaculate housekeeping standards.

"Do you think she knows the meaning of the word *immaculate*?" whispered Mother Millie.

"Clearly not," responded Mother Janie.

A loud and suspicious cough erupted from Mother Janie as Mother Millie belted out a short laugh. The looks on their faces revealed they were trying hard not to laugh. Finally Mother Mae, in a soft and gentle tone, jumped in and told Miss Lillian that they had come today out of concern for the events that transpired yesterday and wanted to make sure she was okay.

Mother Kellie went on to say, "Miss Lillian, we have never seen you as upset as you were yesterday. Can you tell us what happened?"

Miss Lillian twitched her head to the left and scratched it, saying, "Mother Kellie, I am so tired of being disrespected by the men at One Way. Specifically that evil Deacon Evans and crazy Deacon King. They make me feel like crap, the way they trample all over me with their hurtful words. I have had enough, and now that I have worked up the courage to fight back, they have a problem with me. I have sacrificed my entire life for One Way. Since the age of nineteen, I have passed up husbands, dates, and trips to the Caribbean and Italy because of my commitment to One Way."

"Girl, stop!" hollered Mother Karen.

"Are you laughing at me?" asked Miss Lillian as she scooted to the edge of her chair.

Raising her eyebrows while thinking this child was delusional, Mother Janie asked Miss Lillian if she could use her bathroom. Miss Lillian pointed Mother Janie down the long, dark hall to the bathroom. Having used the bathroom earlier, Mother Millie got up and said, "I'll show her where it is."

Miss Lillian looked at the mothers and told them, "I love you mothers because you all have treated me like family since I lost my parents. I will always respect and honor you all."

"Sweetie," Mother Mae said, "you are right not to let no man walk all over you, but handle each situation with grace and tact. Some days we all get tired of those deacons, but as Mother Janie always says, 'You catch more flies with honey than vinegar.' You understand? As far as the sacrifices you have made, I don't know about them, but you can lead a full life as a Christian. You can still marry and be a Christian. You can still date and be a Christian. Look at Mother Kellie and Brother Ben."

Miss Lillian looked at Mother Kellie and started weeping.

Meanwhile, down the hall, Mothers Janie and Millie took a peek behind all the doors, in search of clues. Mother Janie whispered, "I wouldn't put nothing past Miss Lillian. She could be deeply involved in this mess. From my years of watching detective shows, I've learned it's always the one you least suspect."

Mother Millie smiled at Mother Janie and said, "Janie, you know that girl couldn't be caught up in this mess; you know she ain't too bright."

Mother Janie opened the first room past the bathroom and they saw three large beds with dolls and games all over them. In the second room they discovered a bed and a vanity full of wigs, makeup, and jewelry. As Mother Millie stepped into the room, she figured it had to be Miss Lillian's bedroom. As she turned to leave, she saw a huge poster of Pastor Walker on the wall. Mother Millie grabbed Mother Janie and showed her the poster. Mother Janie took one look and dug in her purse for her cell phone to snap a picture. She told Mother Millie to shut the door and hit the light switch so she could get a better shot of the poster.

Mother Janie whispered to Mother Millie, "That child is a hot mess. While Lulabelle and Deacon Evans were trying to get rid of Pastor Walker, Miss Lillian is up in here fantasizing about him."

They both decided that this was just too freaky and that they needed to leave. They turned around and found notes taped to the back of Miss Lillian's bedroom door with her name written as *Mrs. Lillian Walker, Pastor's Wife.* It was written more than ten different times in several shades of ink.

Mother Janie stepped back and asked, "What kind of foolishness is going on up in here?" She snapped a picture of the back of the door as well.

Mother Janie made it to the bathroom and hit the light, and then she immediately turned and made her way down the hall. She told Mother Millie, "If you think I was going to use that bathroom with all those pictures of dead folks hanging on them walls watching me, you must be crazy. Anybody living like this got to be psycho."

Back in the living room Mother Kellie was consoling Miss Lillian. She asked Miss Lillian what was making her cry.

As she pushed Mother Kellie's arm off her shoulder, Miss Lillian blurted, "Here I am in my fifties, and I have never been married. I have been praying for the last thirty years for the Lord to send me a husband, a date, a companion, a sugar daddy, even a man recently released from prison, or a man seeking a green card, any man … and here you are two exits from death, about to get married a second time. How fair is that to me? I feel like I have been cursed. I know I am a much better catch than you on your best day! And no man is even looking my way. Every man I approach says the same thing: 'Let's be friends in the Lord.'"

"Excuse me?" Mother Kellie said. "Child, this better be some twisted joke."

Mother Mae grabbed Mother Kellie's hand and whispered, "Let's not forget we are here to console Miss Lillian."

Mother Kellie shook her head. "Mother Mae, I just endured those insults. No sane man in his right mind should be looking at Miss Lillian until she gets help." Then Mother Kellie moved back to her chair and didn't mumble another word.

Mother Mae told Miss Lillian, "You need to get in touch with your feminine side, honey. No man will give you a second look if you are looking ten to twenty years older than your age. Your makeup, hair, and clothing are way outdated."

"Amen!" echoed Mother Kellie as Mothers Janie and Millie returned to their seats.

As Mother Mae continued, the other mothers nodded in support of her observations.

Mother Janie interrupted, "Miss Lillian, come with me to the coat closet door."

As they stood in front of the mirror hanging on the outside of the door, the other mothers twisted in their seats to see what was going on.

Standing behind Miss Lillian with her hands on her shoulders as they both stared into the mirror, Mother Janie said, "Get a good look of yourself from head to toe."

"Yes, ma'am," said Miss Lillian as she tilted her chin up and looked herself up and down in the mirror.

"Now close your eyes. Picture yourself without the wig, without the drawn-in eyebrows, without the fire-engine-red lipstick and blush, without the granny stockings and shoes, and without the oversized and outdated clothes. Now picture in your mind a new Miss Lillian with a full makeover from head to toe. Nice haircut, color, and style … nicely applied makeup, of course with age-appropriate colors … and a nicely fitted suit and high-heel shoes from one of those nice high-end department stores at the mall in Cincinnati."

Miss Lillian gasped. "Oh my God! I am worthy of this dream. I see the new and improved Miss Lillian!"

Mother Millie whispered, "I can't even get a visual in my mind of Miss Lillian without the drawn-in eyebrows and that awful lipstick that she uses as blush and sometimes as eye shadow. Ugh!"

"It's a dream. It's a pretend game," Mother Addie whispered, even as she smiled and hoped this would be the breakthrough for Miss Lillian.

After several minutes of Miss Lillian smiling and gazing at the mirror with her eyes closed, Mother Janie massaged her shoulders and asked, "Miss Lillian, now tell me, what do you see?"

With her eyes closed and a huge smile on her face, Miss Lillian shrieked in excitement with her hands flapping. "I see Halle Berry! It's Halle Berry that I see."

Her answer stunned the mothers as they looked at each other, shaking their heads.

Still holding Miss Lillian by the shoulders, Mother Janie shook her slightly and asked, "How on God's green earth do you see Halle Berry? Are you blind? Dagummit, open your eyes! How can you go from this to Halle Berry?"

Miss Lillian turned around and faced Mother Janie. "Don't you dare speak to me like that. This is my dream! You're jealous. We all know there is definitely no hope for you to ever get a man. You are trying to relive your youth through me. Get over it!"

"Who do you think you are talking to?" asked Mother Janie.

And the two of them went to arguing.

Unable to get up off the plastic-encased sofa, Mother Mae had to have Mother Kellie and Mother Millie help her up. Mother Mae managed to pull Mother Janie away from Miss Lillian and she whispered, "In one breath you ask her to dream of being someone that she clearly isn't. In the next you scold her for dreaming big. I think you need to calm down and have a seat."

"You're right, Mother Mae," said Mother Janie and then she sat next to Mother Kellie.

Mother Kellie leaned in toward Mother Janie and said, "Miss Lillian has been disrespectful and rude this morning. I don't know this Miss Lillian."

"Don't get me started, Mother Kellie. I am still trying to figure out what happened over there," said Mother Janie as she gestured toward the mirrored coat closet door.

As Mother Millie comforted Miss Lillian, she said, "We really don't know the real Miss Lillian."

"That's right. When I look at you, Miss Lillian, I see your mother and grandmother," said Mother Addie.

Mother Kellie nodded. "Sweetie, it does not help that you wear your mother's wigs and clothing dated back to the sixties and seventies. If you want people to believe you are in your fifties, you need to present yourself as if you are a fifty-year-old woman, not a woman in her eighties or nineties."

"Amen," said many of the mothers.

Miss Lillian rolled her eyes at Mother Kellie, as she figured Mother Kellie owed her that one. She told the mothers she was deeply sorry about what had transpired yesterday and today.

"I didn't mean to insult you, Mother Kellie and Mother Janie. It's menopause. I just started menopause last week."

The mothers shot each other stares of disbelief.

Miss Lillian told them she would issue an apology before the church and a personal apology to Deacon Evans.

Suddenly a large black rat darted across the rug and dashed across the mantle, knocking over pictures. The mothers screamed and pointed at it. Seated with her back toward the mantle, Miss Lillian dived and grabbed the rat. She told the mothers not to panic, as it was her pet hamster, Louie. Then she returned Louie to a cage over in the corner, which the mothers hadn't noticed before.

Mother Janie hollered, "Pet!"

Mother Addie hushed her up, then made her get up and pushed her toward the door. The mothers had seen enough; they began rising and moving toward the front door. Normally the mothers offered prayer before they left from visiting, but this visit abruptly ended with the grabbing of pots and pans, and walking quickly to the front door. So they waved good-bye to Miss Lillian and told her they would be praying for her as they stepped onto the front porch. After they boarded the van, Mother Janie and Mother Millie told the other mothers what they'd found in Miss Lillian's bedroom. Based on everything else they'd witnessed in Miss Lillian's home, the mothers weren't surprised. Mother Mae commented that Miss Lillian was silently screaming for help.

Rotating her finger clockwise around her ear, Mother Janie replied, "Miss Lillian creates things in her mind, and I doubt anything happened. She is so out of touch with reality that it's frightening. You see she called that big rat a hamster."

"Nonetheless something just doesn't sit right with me," said Mother Mae. "Oh well, I just pray this is the end of the Miss Lillian drama."

Mother Kellie shouted, "Don't count on it! When I look into that woman's eyes, I see pain and hurt. Mark my words: there is more to Miss Lillian than meets the eye."

LOST BUT NOW FOUND

The mothers decided to leave the investigation into the whereabouts of Pastor Walker in the capable hands of Frank Mason, and instead just pray about it. They determined they were in over their heads. However, they couldn't help but speculate about their findings. The mothers found themselves sometimes thinking the worst, and so they agreed to stay in prayer and follow Mother Janie's philosophy, which was "No news is good news."

Three weeks after Frank Mason's investigation began, he telephoned Mother Mae and asked how soon he could meet with the Mothers' Board. With excitement in her voice, Mother Mae told Brother Mason that the mothers would be convening at her home the next day at 1:00 p.m. for their weekly prayer meeting and brunch.

"Mother, I will be there at 2:15 p.m. sharp."

"We will see you then."

The next afternoon each time a car door slammed or an engine revved outside, the mothers peered through Mother Mae's front window or her screen door, hoping it was Frank Mason.

Finally Mother Janie asked, "Mothers, why don't we go into a silent prayer until Frank Mason arrives?"

"That's a great idea. That will keep our nerves at bay until he arrives," said Mother Millie.

"I agree," said Mother Mae as she led the mothers back into the dining room.

As the mothers sat around Mother Mae's dining room table, they held hands and bowed their heads for the next twelve minutes. That's when the doorbell rang. They crowded the front door and greeted Frank Mason as Mother Mae welcomed him into her home.

He greeted the mothers with his signature, "Howdy, young ladies."

Normally the mothers would get tickled and blush when Frank would call them "young ladies," but on this occasion the mothers shot him "This is not the time to be playing" stares. Mother Mae instructed Brother Mason to come into the dining room and pull up a chair. As he sat, Mother Janie began to fix him a plate. Brother Mason knew not to argue with the mothers when it came to food. He thanked Mother Janie and then proceeded to pull out his leather notebook.

"Mothers, I have big news. Pastor Walker has been found."

Sighs and smiles filled the room as the mothers listened to Frank. He placed a piece of paper in Mother Mae's hand, and she read it to herself, then exclaimed, "A Christian male correctional facility!" She looked at Frank. "Here in Ohio?"

He just nodded. "What you do with this information is your business. I am not at liberty to discuss any other information related to my investigation until it is completed. When that happens, I will need to present it to you and the entire congregation at the same time, which is in concert with the bylaws of our church. Mothers, I am going to have to go. May I get some foil to wrap my plate?"

"Of course, darling," said Mother Janie.

"Mothers, I will see y'all at church on Sunday."

The mothers waved good-bye to Brother Mason before Mother Mae shut and locked the front door.

"Thank you, Jesus, for Evangelist Hattie," Mother Mae said. "Didn't she tell us that Pastor Walker was in confinement?"

The mothers chimed in with their comments of agreement.

"Oh my, though!" Mother Kellie said. "What crime did Pastor Walker commit to land in prison? Hmm … This would explain why he couldn't continue as pastor. He's been locked up the entire time. This is just sad."

The mothers knew they only had one hour before Deacon King would return to pick them up, so they needed to move fast with what to do with the information from Brother Mason.

"So where is this place in Ohio?" Mother Kellie asked.

Mother Mae read aloud the address from the paper that Brother Mason had given her.

"Oh!" Mother Kellie said. "That's only a hundred miles east of here."

Mother Janie said, "Mothers, we got to go there and see our pastor. We need answers. I don't know how we will get there, but we got to go and represent the Mothers' Board."

"She is right," Mother Mae said. "We won't be able to move forward until we close this chapter."

Mother Mae then told the mothers that only three of them should go, while the rest would stay to attend the prayer luncheon so that no one at the church would become suspicious. Mother Kellie agreed to drive her Mustang since her Corvette couldn't fit three and since she didn't trust her old minivan to make such a lengthy trip. The mothers also decided that Mothers Mae and Janie, the two senior mothers, would accompany her.

Mother Kellie put on her aviator sunglasses and pushed the pedal to the metal as she merged onto the highway. At times the speedometer showed eighty-five miles per hour, but mostly she kept it a steady seventy-five. Mother Janie ate or slept the entire trip, as she had packed a picnic basket of food that included fried chicken, salmon patties, and homemade rolls. Mother Mae stayed quiet, deep in thought as she kept her eyes on the road.

Soon Mother Kellie said, "Mothers, we should be there in the next fifteen minutes."

Mother Kellie was right on the money. As the mothers approached the city limits, Mother Kellie pulled into the local IGA parking lot.

Mother Kellie said, "Mothers, let's pause for a moment of prayer."

Mother Janie led the mothers in prayer, and then they got out of the Mustang with each other's help to stretch their legs. As they walked into the grocery store to use the restroom, they reflected with each other on the events that had led them there.

Ten minutes later, after the mothers had pulled up to the security guardhouse at the correctional facility, a guard asked them their business.

"We are here to see our pastor, the Reverend Willie Walker," Mother Mae said. "We represent the Mothers' Board of One Way Church of the Lord in One Way, Ohio. He is an inmate here."

The guard looked at their church ID badges and directed them where to park and what gate to enter through. The mothers left their purses in the trunk and proceeded with their Bibles, and in their starched white suits, they marched to the visitors' gate to check in. Each mother was searched before walking through the metal detector. The mothers were then directed to the chapel prayer room, where they waited patiently to see Pastor Walker.

"Times have changed," Mother Janie said. "Normally we are seated behind glass or in a common area with armed guards everywhere. Maybe the crime Pastor Walker committed is not so serious that they are allowing us to meet him in the chapel."

In another part of the facility, as Pastor Walker stood to dismiss his "What Is Faith?" men's Bible study class, a guard interrupted and told him he had visitors waiting in the chapel prayer room.

Furrowing his eyebrows, Pastor Walker replied, "Who is it?"

The guard shrugged. "I think it's another church looking to be a part of the prison ministry program."

"Thank you," said Pastor Walker. He told his class, "Keep the faith, brothers, until we meet again." He stood at the door and shook each man's hand as he departed the classroom.

Once he shook the last hand, Pastor Walker focused on getting to the chapel prayer room to meet his visitors. Out of habit Pastor Walker took along his Bible, calendar book, and notepad. From past experience he knew that most visitors wanted to be included on the chapel calendar for some type of religious service, program, or outreach effort. He hummed "This Little Light of Mine" as he walked down the hall. When he approached the chapel prayer room, he was overcome with tears. He quietly said, "Lord, why I am crying these tears?"

Only God knew what was about to happen on the other side of that door. Pastor Walker grabbed his handkerchief and headed into the chapel. Once inside, he felt baffled, because he saw no one. He strode to the back of the chapel prayer room, where an office was located, to see if his visitors were seated there. No one. Pastor Walker shook his head and decided to stay in the chapel to wait and pray, figuring that maybe the visitors hadn't actually been processed in yet.

Meanwhile the mothers were leaving the restroom and heading back to the chapel. Soon they heard a familiar voice coming from the chapel. They opened the chapel door and walked in. They saw someone who looked like Pastor Walker from behind, standing in front of the altar and praying to God.

With emotion in his voice, the man who looked like Pastor Walker said, "Bless these men within the prison walls as they seek you. Forgive them of their sins. Lord, use me as you will. Lord, bless all of my co-workers. Bless the good ones and the bad ones. Lord, I am praying for the young men in this prison who do not know their fathers, mothers, brothers, and sisters. Lord, heal their pain and loneliness. Help them in their fight to become good men, faithful men, and righteous men! Lord, I am calling on you, because you are their only hope. They have put their trust in man and this is where it got them. Lord, show 'em right from wrong. Please, Lord, show them how to be good fathers, faithful husbands, honorable sons, and loving brothers. Lord, when that burden becomes too heavy for them to continue carrying, Lord, carry it for them. Lord, thank you for blessing me to be here. I know it was not my choice, but it was your choice. Lord, thank you for granting me the strength to make it through another day. Help me to do your will and be a blessing to these young men. Lord, bless my momma, my brothers, and bless my friends. Lord, bless my enemies too."

As the three mothers stood twenty feet behind him, they knew it was Pastor Walker, and tears began streaming down their faces. They just felt so overcome by Pastor Walker's prayer, as it reminded them of his first visit to One Way and how hard he prayed for One Way's future, whether it included him or not.

The mothers walked toward Pastor Walker as he finished his prayer and pulled his handkerchief out to wipe his tears. When the mothers stood behind him, he turned around, saw them caught up in tears, and shouted "My Lord! My God! Mothers! It's so good to see you all."

The foursome gathered in a group hug for several minutes, and tears flowed again.

When the crying finally stop, Pastor Walker pulled away and asked, "Mothers, is everything okay?"

"Hell no!" Mother Janie said. "Oh, forgive me, Lord … and Pastor. I'm so sorry. But … you know my heart, Pastor Walker. I have truly been praying for the Lord to remove these bad words from my mouth and believe me, I am making progress."

"Are you sure?" asked Pastor Walker with a grin on his face.

They all laughed at Mother Janie.

"Pastor Walker," Mother Mae said, "we sure miss you at One Way."

His grin disappeared. "Mothers, how on God's earth did you find me? I figured this would be the last place anyone would look for me."

"We have our ways, Pastor Walker," said Mother Janie.

Pastor Walker looked down, and then Mother Kellie spoke up and said, "We don't know what happened, but our church is in shambles right now, and we need to know if the problem that caused you to leave can be fixed. We can't move on and start the healing process until we have closure."

Pastor Walker nodded. "I understand, Mothers, but the church was very clear when they told me my services would no longer be needed. I don't want to cause any further harm or headache to One Way, my family, and friends."

Mother Mae immediately sensed that Pastor Walker was trapped in some mess at the hands of either the deacons or the trustees. Either way, she knew Lulabelle had to be involved. Under her breath she asked the Lord to forgive her even as she tried to get more information from Pastor Walker: "Lulabelle provided the church attorney, Frank Mason, and me with a report of what happened, but we really need your side of the story. We are three of the most senior members of One Way, and we also represent the Mothers' Board, so we won't settle for half of the facts; we want all of the facts. So please share with us, what you can, your version of the events that led up to your departure."

Pastor Walker nodded again. "Mothers, come have a seat." He motioned for them to sit on the front pew, while he sat in a folding chair facing them. "Mothers, it all started after that last Sunday sermon I preached. Before I could even get home good, I received an anonymous call on my cell phone, telling me that my momma, brothers, and some of my members' lives would be in jeopardy if I did not leave One Way, Ohio. When I returned home, I found my home in shambles. It had been burglarized and there was also a note attached to my front door. The note told me in so many words that my family's safety and the reputation of One Way would be harmed if I remained at One Way. I know I handled this situation cowardly, but I just didn't know what to do. I prayed and asked God to show me his way, but I moved too quickly.

"Around 5:00 a.m. on the Monday after my last Sunday preaching at One Way, three armed men appeared at my front door and told me that my family, neighbors, and members at One Way were in danger if I stayed. They falsely accused me of beating my former girlfriend and molesting her grandkids. They showed me letters that Mary and her grandkids wrote, and photos of injuries that I supposedly caused.

This information would be presented to One Way, the local newspaper, and to the police. Of course I felt devastated and shocked since this was nothing but lies. I tried to reach Mary Hicks, but her number had been changed and she had moved. I couldn't breathe. It felt like a bad dream. A nightmare. The statement from her—I just can't bring myself to repeat it. It was … graphic. Just lies." Pastor Walker shook his head in disgust.

The mothers sat there, speechless.

"I was told the only way out of this mess would be to immediately leave the church, vacate the house, and leave town. The three armed men offered me $5,000, but I refused it. Mothers, I had to leave. After they left my home, they went to my mother's house and roughed her up and ransacked her home. I felt like Job. I was tired and frustrated, unable to understand why this happened. I decided to come up here, get a motel, and visit my dad's gravesite. When I went to the cemetery to visit my daddy on this facility's grounds, I felt at peace. One day while visiting his grave, the chaplain told me about a teaching job he had in his chapel. Since my heart was heavy and I felt betrayed and forsaken, I needed to be in place where I felt needed, wanted, and embraced. Mothers, do you hear what I am saying? I felt like I was robbed in the middle of the night and abandoned on some dirt road in the country and left for dead. Being an old black man, with little money, living off my modest pension, my family don't have much money, and all I know is preaching God's Word, so I couldn't see my way out of this. I cried many nights and hours. This chapel has been my salvation and my home for the last four months. They gave me shelter, food, clothing. But you know what, Mothers? I have no hate in my heart for One Way. Hate will kill you."

"Sure you're right," said Mother Mae. "Hate is dangerous."

"Reading statements from those seven-, eight-, and nine-year-olds drove me to doubt myself," Pastor Walker said. "I kept wrestling with God and thinking maybe this was not his will and mine alone, but he showed me differently.

"Many of our young black men are unreachable outside of these prison walls. They don't have time or won't make time to learn about Jesus. Inside these walls, they have nothing but time on their hands. When new inmates arrive here, they are broken, confused, miserable, and at rock bottom. Many of these young men don't know their fathers. Some of them don't even know their mothers. They lived with undiagnosed addiction and mental health issues. Some of them ... all they know is a life of hustling and criminal activities. Through the Lord, I am able to share the Word with them. Teach them how to plead for God's forgiveness. I also teach them how to resist temptation, and about the qualities of a good man. All of my classes are full. I can't imagine being anywhere else to serve the Lord. These men are serious about the Word of God. Mothers, this is where God was leading me. I am a firm believer that everything happens for a reason. My being here at this facility is my season; this is what God had destined for me. Through God's Word, all of the men in this facility are given a second chance. It's up to them to accept it. It's my job to present the options: eternal life or condemnation.

"Do you know how many young black men transition through this facility? More than two thousand per year. Some I never see again. Others can't make it out there and come back. I already have many success stories. Many of the released men have written me to express their gratitude and to update me on their lives outside of these walls. That keeps me coming back and giving my all."

"Amazing," said Mother Kellie. "I guess this is where you are supposed to be."

"It's reassuring to know that God is still in the deliverance business," Mother Mae said. "Pastor Walker, I don't know if I was in your shoes if I could have held out and waited on the Lord. I admire your tenacity."

"Mothers, it's time for One Way to move on. It's a new season, Mothers. Go claim it! I know you were hoping for a different outcome, but sometimes what you don't want is what you need. Believe me when I say, change is never easy. It's downright frightening.

Remember this: don't expect a change if you don't make one. It has to start within you!"

As Pastor Walker walked the mothers to the parking lot, they thanked him for his time and told him it was good to see him. They promised they would be in touch once the church had sorted everything out. Pastor Walker didn't respond; he just told them, "God bless each of you and One Way."

The car ride back to One Way was quiet. The mothers were in deep thought about Pastor Walker's revelations. They were having a hard time understanding who would do something so vulgar and wicked and misrepresent the church at the same time. The mothers knew they had to be extremely careful in regard to whom they shared this information with, because they didn't know who all was involved and how deep this mess went.

Mother Kellie finally broke the ice and said, "Mothers, is it possible somebody or somebodies from One Way would be capable of such deceit and sinful ways?"

Mother Janie replied, "Oh, yes, my sister. We are going to have to fast and pray on this matter. This is corruption. Pastor Walker's job was taken from him. Someone at One Way decided they were the judge and jury on this one, and I ain't happy about it!"

Mother Mae told Mother Janie that she hit it on the nail.

Mother Kellie said, "Mothers, we have an enemy in our church that is working against the church to divide and deceive One Way. Psalm 101:7 tells us that 'He that worketh deceit shall not dwell within my house: he that telleth lies shall not tarry in my sight.' Mothers, we can't sit idle and allow these deceitful folks full latitude over One Way."

"What a crying shame," Mother Mae said. "Mothers, I will contact Frank Mason as soon as I get home and update him on our visit with Pastor Walker."

After arriving home, Mother Mae grabbed her phone and called Brother Mason, then told him everything.

"Mother Mae, I am so glad you called and provided me an update of your visit with Pastor Walker. With that information in hand, I now have news for you as well."

Brother Mason informed her that he was bringing his investigation to a close and he was ready to report his findings to the congregation in a meeting to be held Saturday at 9:00 a.m. in the church's fellowship hall.

Mother Mae thanked him for the call and told him she and the mothers looked forward to seeing him Saturday. Then, overcome with excitement, Mother Mae managed to calmly call each of the mothers and inform them of the upcoming meeting.

DARKNESS TO LIGHT

The casually dressed congregation sat anxiously on this sunny and calm Saturday morning. Unbeknownst to the 523 folks sitting in the fellowship hall, Frank Mason, One Way member and assistant district attorney for the local county court, and his wife, Deputy Mildred Mason, of the One Way sheriff's department, were prepared for the unexpected, even if that meant making an arrest.

Miss Lillian was seated at a table up front, recording the minutes of this meeting. Evangelist Hattie was seated next to her. Behind them sat the deacons and trustees. The mothers were seated behind the deacons and trustees. The rest of the congregation were seated in folding chairs behind the mothers.

As everyone sat there, staring at each other while trying to figure out who knew what and what was about to happen, Brother Frank Mason emerged on stage and greeted the crowd. He thanked everyone for coming out to hear his report relative to Pastor Walker's departure. Brother Mason then read Leviticus 6:1-5. Many in the congregation opened their Bibles to follow him as he read:

> "And the Lord spake unto Moses, saying,
>   "If a soul sin, and commit a trespass against the
> Lord, and lie unto his neighbour in that which was

delivered him to keep, or in fellowship, or in a thing
taken away by violence, or hath deceived his neighbour;

"Or have found that which was lost, and lieth con-
cerning it, and sweareth falsely; in any of all these that
a man doeth, sinning therein:

"Then it shall be, because he hath sinned, and is
guilty, that he shall restore that which he took violently
away, or the thing which he hath deceitfully gotten, or
that which was delivered him to keep, or the lost thing
which he found,

"Or all that about which he hath sworn falsely; he
shall even restore it in the principal, and shall add the
fifth part more thereto, and give it unto him to whom
it appertaineth, in the day of his trespass offering."

After Brother Mason offered a prayer, he dove right into his report:
"As you all know, several months ago our church was paralyzed by
the news of Pastor Walker's sudden disappearance. After weeks and
months of receiving letters, e-mails, and telephone calls from the
church membership and friends, I decided to hire a private investi-
gator to look into the matter to make sure there was no wrongdoing
on the part of One Way. I am sorry that I couldn't share this with
any of you, but we did not want the investigation compromised in
any way.

"In addition to learning, much to my surprise, that a few members
sitting before me actually detested Pastor Walker, and everything he
stood for, the vast majority of us found Pastor Walker to be a great
leader and teacher. Pastor Walker's sudden exit was difficult to understand. Here was a man who loved his job, valued his position, and
loved this church. Why would he walk away from it all in the middle
of the night? No phone call. No note. Nothing."

As Brother Mason walked from one side of the stage to the other,
the congregation followed his footsteps as his leather shoes tapped
the hardwood floor that covered the stage.

"How could he move from his home, disconnect his home and cell phone numbers, and not phone the church, the deacons, or his dedicated secretary? It's like he disappeared into thin air. After we all sat here on that fateful Sunday morning when the deacons delivered the sad news, many of us were overcome with grief, while a few others knew exactly what happened to Pastor Walker, and they continued to play the part for months to come.

"What would drive a man to abandon his church, home, and friends? That is the question that has been nagging me for months. I always figured someone sitting within the congregation on that awful day knew all about the events surrounding Pastor Walker's departure. But to anticipate something, and then see it actually take place, is the difference between a nightmare and reality.

"At the hands of a few members seated before me today, Pastor Walker was wrongfully terminated, bribed, and falsely removed as a member. He had his home ransacked, was forcibly removed from his own home, and sustained physical and mental abuse. His mother was assaulted and her home was also ransacked. "

Taking notes, Miss Lillian shook her head as she uttered, "What a crying shame!"

Deacon Evans rubbed Lulabelle's shoulder as they both looked dazed after hearing Brother Mason's remarks.

"Members," Brother Mason went on, "a pink decorative mug with the letter 'L' on it was discovered in Pastor Walker's home."

Miss Lillian turned and looked at Lulabelle. This caused people seated near her to do the same.

Brother Mason continued. "The reason this mug bears much significance is because after Pastor Walker disappeared, the property management company took pictures of the house after it was professionally cleaned."

On the big screen in the front of the fellowship hall, Brother Mason displayed pictures of Pastor Walker's house. The photos were date-stamped to show when the professional cleaning had taken place. The next picture was date-stamped a week later from the previous photos, showing the decorative pink mug sitting on the countertop in Pastor Walker's home. The next photo showed an empty strawberry diet soda can in the trash bin. The next photo showed the soda can placed on the countertop for closer scrutiny.

Brother Mason calmly gazed into the congregation and said, "Members, here is another clue left behind. Somebody sitting in this building knows someone who drinks this type of soda. Speak up; don't be afraid to tell the truth. Look closely at this photo."

Deacon Evans' mouth fell open. He looked at Lulabelle and whispered, "Oh my God!"

"Why are you looking at me like that, Harold?" Lulabelle whispered back.

Brother Mason continued. "So someone returned to the house, looking for something they must have left behind that would have incriminated them. They returned and were sloppy to leave this mug and soda can. Or maybe they deliberately left this evidence. It hurts my heart to report that the fingerprint analysis proves that the person or persons who left the pink decorative mug and soda can are seated here today. In addition, my investigators returned to the former home of Pastor Walker, and we took fingerprint analysis from the kitchen faucet, from the icemaker and water buttons on the refrigerator, and from the countertop where the mug was found. We found so many members' fingerprints that we had to conduct several undercover operations."

The congregation, including Deacon Evans, all looked toward Lulabelle, who hollered, "As God is my witness, I don't own a nasty pink mug, and I have never stepped foot into Pastor Walker's home. If that mug has my fingerprints on it, then it's a setup. You hear me, a setup!" she shouted and shook her head in anger.

Deacon Evans sighed as he shifted in his seat.

As Brother Mason paused to sip some water, Mother Mae whispered to Mother Kellie, "I just can't believe it's Lulabelle; she can be mean but this isn't her style."

Mother Kellie nodded in agreement.

Mother Janie whispered in Mother Mae's ear, "You think he's talking about Lulabelle?"

"Mother Mae, I don't have a clue, and it's killing me that he is dragging this on and on."

Brother Mason put down his water and said, "Pastor Walker was threatened with the following false allegations. Members, it sickens me to have to report these facts, but I have a duty to God and One Way to bring these facts forward. The letter I am about to read will speak to the false allegations of blackmail, assault, and domestic violence assigned to Pastor Walker by person or persons seated before me this morning. We will also post a copy of the letter on the screen in front of you.

"'Dear Mr. Mason,

At your request, I am writing this letter to set the record straight about Willie Walker. I have known Pastor Walker for more than ten years, and during that time he has always treated my children, grandchildren, and me with care and the utmost respect. When I think back to all the men I have had in and out of my life and in my children's lives, and the beatings, abuse, and mistreatment me and my family endured over my poor choice in men, I know now that Pastor Walker was good for me and my family. I was greedy and wanted more than he had to give. When I think back over the years, I was no prize to be around, but he never judged me even when I made bad decisions. He was always lending a helping hand. He never asked for anything in return. He helped me to get my GED at fifty years of age. I had no desire to do this until Pastor Walker came into my life. I finally learned how to read and research the Bible with his help. He was truly a blessing to my family. He baptized all of my children and got them involved in church.

And then to thank him for everything, I betrayed him. I am so hurt by my actions that played a part in his removal from One Way. I allowed myself to be manipulated by a few bad apples at One Way, but then I turned around and manipulated my own grandchildren by asking them to lie on Pastor Walker. All he ever did for my grandchildren was love them. The bruises shown in the photographs taken by representatives of One Way were self-inflicted. The letters my grandchildren wrote were false. They were instructed to write the letters by me and representatives of One Way. Two of my three grandchildren understood the words they wrote and were very hurt by them. I have to look at my grandchildren every day, and I always wonder what they think of their treacherous grandmother. It hurts my heart to know that I allowed myself to sink this low.

I ruined a man's life over a small portion of money, just $5,000. When people say money is the root of evil, I know it now to be true. Mr. Mason, I did wrong and I am truly sorry. I don't believe I am worthy to step foot into a sanctuary after the awful things I put your church and Pastor Walker through. As I muster up the courage to finish this letter, I ask the Lord to have mercy on my soul and to elevate One Way to higher grounds, because I conspired and did wrong to people who did nothing but love me and pray for me. I am also praying that the Lord will bless Pastor Walker. One Way Church, I am so sorry.
Sincerely,
Mary Hicks'"

Brother Mason looked at the faces of the shocked congregation and then continued. "Clearly, Mary Hicks is devastated about the role she played in the mess. She knew the letters she and her grandchildren wrote were to be used in a blackmail scheme to get rid of Pastor Walker. She was given $2,500 after the letters were written and another $2,500 after Pastor Walker left One Way. My investigators and I have spoken with her, and she will now come forward." With that, Brother Mason nodded toward the rear of the hall.

The members twisted and turned in their seats to get a glimpse of this woman named Mary Hicks. As Brother Mason waved the slender, bright-skinned woman dressed in a navy pantsuit up front, the members sat in silence, awed that a nice-looking woman would play such a part. Everyone was trying to get a good look at her to see if they recognized this woman. Whispers and stares came from every corner of the fellowship hall as Mary Hicks came forward.

Mother Janie whispered into Mother Mae's ear, "At least she is a decent-looking woman. I can't wait to hear what she is about to say."

Mother Mae nodded.

Finally, Mary was up front. She shook Brother Mason's hand as he asked her to name the people who had asked her to participate in this scam. Mary, her hair up in a bun and looking contrite, addressed the church with an apology. With emotion choking her voice, Mary said, "I was desperate and, yes, bitter about Pastor Walker choosing the church over me. I felt him taking this job here at One Way meant that he would meet and marry a smart, churchgoing woman."

Mary choked up between sobs about how sorry she was and how she hoped the Lord would forgive her. She then said that late one night a woman called her at the request of Pastor Walker. The woman said that he had wanted her to meet the dumb woman he'd dumped. Mary said the woman told her that she herself had since dumped Reverend Walker, and she wanted her to know how badly Pastor Walker was talking about her and her illegitimate grandchildren.

Mary said, "I was hopping mad. Of course I wanted to meet this woman because I thought she was my friend after she said she dumped Pastor Walker and he started talking bad about me. Instead of me calming down and thinking about the good God-fearing man I knew Willie—excuse me, Pastor Walker—to be, I let this woman, someone I had never met, influence me to partake in her scheme. Later I learned that Pastor Walker had never said any of those awful things about my family and me. That woman came up with these lies to use me in her scheme to get back at Pastor Walker for rejecting her. I feel so bad right now. I don't even feel worthy to be in your presence, church members." Mary paused and wiped tears from her eyes.

"Brother Mason, the woman that came to my house in the middle of the night with a six-pack of beer is here. She told me her name and I will never forget it. Her name is Lulabelle. Ms. Lulabelle, I will not let you get away with ruining Willie Walker's good name, assaulting his momma and inflicting pain on this church!"

The crowd erupted with gasps, whispers, murmurs, and even some shouts of "No, Lord!"

Panic twisted Lulabelle's face. She looked at Deacon Evans and whispered, "That woman is a liar. I will not be persecuted by some harlot trying to extort money from our church."

Unsure what to say, Deacon Evans asked Lulabelle, "Okay, can you explain what is going on? Do you know that woman? Give me something to believe."

A sobbing Lulabelle whispered, "No, I can't, because I am not involved. I have never ever seen that woman before."

"Jesus, Lulabelle, I don't know what to believe," Deacon Evans whispered.

Brother Mason pulled Mary back and asked her, "Are you sure it was Lulabelle Evans?"

Mary nodded. "Yes, I am absolutely sure. She is sitting right over there." Mary pointed in the general direction of Lulabelle and Deacon Evans.

Now Lulabelle rose from her seat and shouted to Mary, "You are a liar and the truth is not in you. I know I am not perfect. Yes, I am a sinner! I know I am not the easiest person to get along with, but I love One Way and would never violate or exploit my position."

Mary motioned toward Brother Mason and said, "No no no! *That woman* is not Lulabelle Evans." She pointed a bit closer and shouted,

"*That* is the woman that came to my house and said her name was Lulabelle Evans!"

As the members strained to see who Mary was pointing out, Brother Mason looked at Mary and asked her if she was she absolutely sure that she was identifying the right woman.

Mary responded, "On my momma's grave … *that* is the woman that came to my house offering me $5,000 in cash."

She was pointing at none other than Miss Lillian, who sat stock still, her face ashen.

Lulabelle stepped forward, grabbed Miss Lillian by the neck, and began hitting her. Miss Lillian rose up from her seat and pulled away as Deacon Evans grabbed Lulabelle and held her back. Brother Mason first had Mary Hicks leave the room, then motioned for his wife to keep a close eye on Miss Lillian where she sat, already back to taking notes.

Once all the commotion had calmed, Brother Mason continued. "Members, we located Pastor Walker. Yes, we did, and had a long talk with him. He confided that he is at peace in his present location and wishes that we withhold his whereabouts until we have resolved this matter. I must tell you Pastor Walker was deeply hurt by the entire ordeal. He and his family have obviously suffered from the damage done by folks sitting within these walls."

Mother Janie whispered to Mother Mae, "Oh my Jesus, how could there be more to this tragic story?"

Mother Mae touched Mother Janie's hand and shook her head.

Brother Mason hushed the crowd and continued. "Pastor Walker was unable to identify or name the persons responsible for this incident. So after we researched all of the facts that were provided by him, his mother, his neighbors, and many of you honest members, we were able to trace this calculated misdeed back to none other than our very own—"

But before he could get the name out, a loud and frightening scream erupted from the front of the hall. It started as a wail, and then erupted into an uncanny laugh—from Miss Lillian. Folks seated on the front row scattered quickly to the rear of the hall. Evangelist Hattie, half asleep, remained seated next to where Miss Lillian sat. Evangelist Hattie woke all the way up and smiled at Miss Lillian, unsure of what had just happened. She turned around, looked behind them, and saw the congregation staring at her.

Evangelist Hattie whispered to Miss Lillian, "Child, what is going on up in here?"

"I don't have a clue, Evangelist Hattie," said Miss Lillian.

Miss Lillian buried her head in her notebook and continued writing. Meanwhile Evangelist Hattie dozed off again.

Deacon Evans whispered to the other deacons, "I knew something wasn't right with that woman."

Mother Millie looked at the mothers and told them, "I told you she wasn't wrapped too tight. I knew she had a thing for Pastor Walker. Remember the writing on the back of her bedroom door? That was our clue that she was obsessed with that man."

The congregation looked stunned as they kept their eyes on who they believed to be the most faithful church member and eloquent speaker, their very own Miss Lillian, who was literally having a nervous breakdown right before her fellow church members.

Brother Mason went on. "Members, Miss Lillian had created in her mind a fictitious relationship between herself and Pastor Walker at the urging of several other members."

Mother Mae motioned at Mother Kellie. "This must stop! He shouldn't continue with this in Miss Lillian's presence. This is not good."

Miss Lillian then started up again with her hollow, bone-chilling laugh. Evangelist Hattie, again startled from sleep by Miss Lillian's shrilling laugh, inhaled deeply as she tried to figure out what was going on. As she looked around and saw the deacons and trustees had cleared the table behind them, she smiled at Miss Lillian before grabbing her purse and Bible and moving to the empty table behind them.

Brother Mason continued. "Given Miss Lillian's fragile state, she was not acting alone in this ordeal; she was used as a pawn. Someone encouraged Miss Lillian to feel betrayed by Pastor Walker's actions. That person urged her to get even by using the information he gave her against him. In addition this person persuaded her that if she couldn't have him, no one else at One Way should be able to have him, not even the congregation as a whole. In addition to Miss Lillian already being sore about Mother Kellie's upcoming marriage, this person brainwashed Miss Lillian into believing that God slighted her on being the next bride at One Way. So to prevent Mother Kellie from getting married, she had to get rid of Pastor Walker. She already knew that Brother Ben and Mother Kellie only wanted Pastor Walker to marry them."

Still laughing, Miss Lillian suddenly rose up and belted out another scream at the top of her lungs. "I hate all of you, especially both of you!" said Miss Lillian as she turned and pointed at Deacon Evans and Lulabelle.

"The feeling is mutual," shouted Deacon Evans as he held Lulabelle's hand.

"Harold, shut up!" whispered Lulabelle.

"All of you mistreated me!" Miss Lillian said. "You knew I had nobody, and you laughed at me, made fun of me, and never embraced me when all of my family passed on. Brother Mason, you stand before the church and persecute me. You're talking as if I am not here. Newsflash! I am right here! The only thing I may be guilty of is being in love with someone who doesn't love me."

Brother Mason nodded at her, and then motioned for her to step up onto the stage.

Miss Lillian did so and addressed the congregation: "Have you ever loved someone so badly? I mean loved hard? Gave your all and never asked for anything in return … just love, simple love? I gave my last dime for love and got rejected. Not once, but every time I tried, I was rejected. So call me crazy or disturbed, but I did this for love. Maybe I never learned the proper way to show love or receive love, but I tried my best. Each time One Way, the members, and the pastors shut me out. I was never good enough. I was never pretty enough.

I was always lacking in some way. That's how you all made me feel Sunday after Sunday."

The congregation seemed stunned by Miss Lillian's comments, and everyone remained quiet.

"You people call yourselves Christians," Miss Lillian went on. "Well, Christians wouldn't make me feel isolated and alone in the church, but you all did. Pastor Walker didn't know how good of a woman I was. It was his loss. On that late Sunday night when we were discussing the calendar, I pleaded with him to give me a chance or tell me how I could improve my chances, but he kept saying that the only women in his life were Mary Hicks and his mother. He was going to pay. How dare he lead me on by touching my hand, winking at me in meetings, and calling me at home? I knew he wanted me, but his momma kept getting in the way, and I tried to tell him that he was nothing but a momma's boy. I told him he would pay for this. He acted clueless. He said, 'Miss Lillian, what on God's earth are you talking about?' But I saw right through his act."

Standing there before the congregation, Miss Lillian pulled off her wig, kicked off her shoes, and began to scratch her skin.

The congregation looked petrified.

Miss Lillian then shouted, "I did it! I paid that woman to lie about Pastor Walker because he had it coming. I paid those men to go and ransack Pastor Walker's home, to rough up his mother and ransack her home as well, and then to move Pastor Walker out of that house. Pastor Walker disrespected me and my friends, so I got even."

A careful Brother Mason turned toward Miss Lillian and asked her calmly, "Miss Lillian, whom else did Pastor Walker disrespect?"

Miss Lillian gave Brother Mason a hideous frown and whispered, "Pastor Walker wouldn't loan Clara Mae the money she needed to avoid eviction, and he wronged her. So I told her about Mary Hicks and she said she would handle the rest."

In the very back Clara Mae stood up and shouted, "It wasn't just me! If I am going down, so are you, Deacon Larry Miller."

Everyone turned around, shocked to see Clara Mae.

"She come back for this, knowing she was guilty?" Mother Mae said to Mother Kellie.

But Mother Kellie just shrugged. "Thought she was gone for good after that call to Janie."

Clara Mae ranted on, pointing up front at Deacon Miller to make sure he didn't leave her to shoulder the blame. "Deacon Miller hated Pastor Walker. He had it in for Pastor Walker from day one, but he was a coward to do it by himself so he dragged Miss Lillian and me in on this. He was the mastermind behind this scheme. He did not like Pastor Walker coming up in here changing things. He didn't like the Bible training, and he didn't like how Pastor Walker kissed up to the Mothers' Board. When you folks went to investigate, he cleaned up behind himself to make sure no clues would be found. He deliberately left that pink mug to draw attention elsewhere. When Miss Lillian and I tried to tell him we wanted out, he blackmailed us. He made Miss Lillian bankroll the operation, plus pay him monthly until a new pastor was named."

Deacon Miller rose and shouted for Clara Mae to shut up. He then accused Lillian and Clara Mae of being desperate liars. Then, suddenly, Deacon Miller tried to make a run for the church exit, but he was apprehended by Usher Gibson and Deacon Carter and brought up front.

Deacon Miller shouted, "I have always hated this church. I don't know why I stayed this long."

Deacon Carter seated Deacon Miller in front of the mothers. Clara Mae continued explaining how Deacon Miller kept pushing them to keep everything going, and how he became increasingly upset when the Mothers' Board decided to look into Pastor Walker's departure.

Deacon Miller turned behind him and told the mothers in a demeaning tone, "You nosey old maids should have minded your own business. Nobody got hurt or killed, so I don't see the problem."

Mother Janie leaned over to Deacon Miller as she gripped her Bible and whispered into his ear, "You need to check yourself, Deacon Miller. God don't like ugly."

"Mother Janie, please!" Deacon Miller grunted.

Mother Janie then stood and shouted, "Satan, I rebuke thee."

Deacon Miller looked up at Mother Janie and told her to back off before she got knocked down.

Mother Janie raised her Bible in the air and beat Deacon Miller over the head with it as she shouted, "I rebuke thee, Satan. Get thee out of here. In the name of Jesus, I rebuke thee!"

From the congregation came an unfamiliar voice, singing, "Trouble in my way, I have to cry sometimes, trouble in my way, I have to cry sometimes. I lie awake at night, but that's all right, 'cause I know Jesus will fix it after a while." It was Lulabelle, who stood up with tears in her eyes, singing the song her late father always sang as he led devotional service.

The room sat in silence, frozen, as they watched a broken Lulabelle stand before them, praising the Lord. Brother Mason's wife removed Miss Lillian, Clara Mae, and Deacon Miller from the fellowship hall as the remaining members stood and joined Lulabelle in song.

In the foyer behind the fellowship hall, Brother Mason's wife was trying to sort it all out. Mother Mae and Mother Janie came back to help. Mother Mae went to a sobbing Miss Lillian and held her in her arms.

Mother Mae whispered, "Miss Lillian, I have always loved you as a daughter. I am so sorry. I never meant to hurt you."

Miss Lillian stared into Mother Mae's eyes. She knew Mother Mae was sincere and she rested her head on Mother Mae's shoulder as she began sobbing.

Mother Mae patted her on the back and whispered, "Baby, it's okay. One Way loves you and we understand. There, there, just let it out."

Back in the fellowship hall, Brother Mason handed the microphone to Mother Kellie. Mother Kellie was visibly shaken but managed to say, "Good morning, members. I am so at a loss for words, but I know God will make a way. He will heal us from this nightmare. Let's keep Miss Lillian and Clara Mae in prayer. Miss Lillian's condition is a result of years of being alone, teased, and mistreated. The results today could have been quite different—even tragic. She has been a member of this big church for all of her life, but, as she put it, always felt isolated and alone in the midst of her church family and friends."

Getting more emotional, Mother Kellie shouted, "Fellow brothers and sisters, that should never happen in church. This means we are not on top of our game, as the young folks declare. We are slipping. We have to really work on loving each other. As Mother Mae often puts it, 'Don't tell me what you going to do. Show me!' We have to show each other love. Don't take for granted that seeing each other on Sunday and Wednesday is enough. Many of us live alone and don't have regular contact with our families, but we got each other. Pick up the phone and call somebody. You don't have to spend an hour on the phone. With a new pastor coming on board, we got to do better. Well … I'm sorry, I know I need to stop preaching."

"Go on and preach, Mother Kellie," shouted Deacon Evans, which shocked not only Mother Kellie, but also the Mothers' Board.

"Members," Mother Kellie said, "I am going to turn the microphone over to Evangelist Hattie, as she has an announcement that Brother Mason asked her to read to us."

Mother Kellie handed Evangelist Hattie the microphone, but Evangelist Hattie waved her away and lifted her personal 18-karat-gold wireless microphone even as Mothers Mae and Janie came back in and sat down.

She mumbled, "Testing one, two, three" as she tapped the microphone to make sure it was on. After untangling the string around her neck that held three pairs of glasses, she placed the first pair on and huffed. She removed them, placed the second pair on, and smiled as she began to read the note handed to her by Brother Mason.

"Members of One Way, I am proud to announce that Reverend Bernie Hall has been selected as our next pastor. He has accepted the position and is prepared to start next Sunday, which will be our 100th church anniversary. For those of you who are not aware, Reverend Hall comes to us from Chicago. He will bring along his lovely wife, Robin Hall. They have four grown children who live in Mobile, San Diego, Seattle, and Miami. They also will be accompanying Reverend Hall next week. Please show them love and respect. We want them to feel welcome and stay a very long time, as this is our prayer."

Mother Mae stood up and asked everybody to gather up front for prayer. Tears flowed endlessly as Mother Janie led prayer.

During the ride home the mothers were quiet as Deacon King had the song "Trouble in My Way" playing from the CD player.

Finally Mother Janie spoke up and said, "I still can't believe Clara Mae and Miss Lillian were involved in this mess. You know, I used to babysit that nappy-headed Larry Miller. I always knew he was up go no good. He told us from the start he had been in Pastor Walker's home. Remember his report: 'Members, every room, closet, and cupboard in that house was empty.' How would he have known that? Isn't it strange how things work out, because I was sure it had to be Lulabelle. I just never saw this coming."

"I hear you, Mother Janie," Mother Addie said. "I doubt that I will be able to sleep tonight, because things sure got spooky today."

Mother Millie jumped in next: "I knew something strange was going on with Miss Lillian. That girl should have been committed years ago. You see how she keeps her house. And the poster of Pastor Walker and the writing on the back of her bedroom door. Mothers, the signs were all up in our faces, and we couldn't see them. I feel bad for her, but I pray she gets the help she so desperately needs. She's young and has time to recover."

Mother Mae shook her head, feeling both sorrow and shame. "You are so right, Mother Millie. The signs were there. She was reaching out, but we were blinded by her cries because our focus was on the wrong things."

Meanwhile, Deacon Evans sobbed as he drove Lulabelle home. "Lu, I am so sorry that I doubted you. I hope you can forgive me. The evidence kept stacking up, and when that woman called your name out, I just lost it."

Lulabelle, still humming "Trouble in My Way," gently stroked Deacon Evans' arm as he drove. "Harold, it's going to be okay. I forgive you. Today I learned something about faith and myself: God is able to bring you through heartache and pain. No matter if its self-inflicted, caused by others, or if you inflict it upon someone. Just let God do it. Stop pretending that you fixed it and let God fix it."

100TH CHURCH ANNIVERSARY

You would have thought the Oscars were being held at One Way Church of the Lord with all the furs, lace, diamonds, trendy suits, and dresses on display in the congregation on its 100th anniversary. The congregation felt so proud of this day, especially considering the journey it had taken to make it to this day.

With 612 people sitting in the congregation, Deacon Evans, fired up with the Holy Spirit, came forward to present One Way's new pastor. In an enthusiastic and joyful tone, Deacon Evans shouted, "Good morning, members and friends! Today is our church's 100th anniversary. We have been through the storm for the last several months, but God made a way for One Way. We are all witnesses to his existence, his greatness, and his mercy. Let's give him praise this morning."

The members jumped to their feet, rejoicing.

Deacon Evans continued. "One Way members, I present our new pastor, Pastor Bernie Hall."

After thunderous applause and a standing ovation, Pastor Hall, his wife, and children made their way up front. Evangelist Hattie greeted him and welcomed him. The new first family then took their seats on the first row. At the podium Pastor Hall thanked the congregation and gave honor to his wife and children before proceeding with his sermon.

"Church, today we are going to discuss asking for forgiveness! Too many of us take the easy way out of dilemmas with a quick 'I'm sorry,' or a lazy and quiet, 'Sorry.' But today, church, we are going to talk about asking our brothers and sisters for forgiveness—looking them in the eye and waiting for their responses. Open your Bibles and if you don't have one, raise your hand, and an usher will deliver you one promptly."

Pastor Hall pointed Usher Gibson to the choir box, as several members in the choir were without Bibles. With lipstick, not only on her lips, but also on her chin and mustache area, a smiling Usher Gibson quickly distributed the Bibles.

After seeing no more hands in the air, Pastor Hall proceeded in a loud and commanding voice: "Church, turn with me to Luke 6:37 and 38. Verse 37 reads as follows, 'Judge not, and ye shall not be judged: condemn not, and ye shall not be condemned: forgive, and ye shall be forgiven,' and now to Verse 38: 'Give, and it shall be given unto you; good measure, pressed down, and shaken together, and running over, shall men give into your bosom. For with the same measure that ye mete withal it shall be measured to you again.'"

Pastor Hall closed his Bible and dabbed his forehead with his handkerchief. He removed his reading glasses and left the pulpit area. As he walked down the steps of the stage to the front of the sanctuary, he positioned himself in front of a standing microphone.

"One Way, this is our season. This moment, this day, this month, and this year is our time to ask for forgiveness. We would be foolish to think that we as a church can move forward in this new era without correcting our errors. We as a church must be on the same page at the same time. I prayed about it, and God wanted me to do this so that we can stop the bleeding and pain we have inflicted in those that have been hurt. We don't need to rehash what was said and done in the past, but today on this 100th church anniversary, we are going to right our wrongs, confess our sins, and move forward in the name of Jesus!"

Pastor Hall moved to the mothers' bench, where he slapped their pew and shouted, "Are you with me, church?"

It sent a jolt down the Mother's Board pew that made them jump, but drove the congregation wild as everyone stood, shouting in agreement.

Pastor Hall moved back to the podium, bobbing and weaving side to side, and said, "Pastor Willie Walker and Mother Aretha Walker, come on up here, right now!"

The surprised congregation turned to the rear of the sanctuary and saw Pastor Walker making his way up front, holding the hand of his mother. Pastor Walker was dressed in a black suit with a gray-and-white tie, and Mrs. Walker wore a gray two-piece suit, with matching pumps and a stunning gray hat. The congregation hushed as their eyes fixated on Pastor Walker and his mother making their way up front, passing by pew after pew and extending waves to the members. Members got caught up in the moment, crying, smiling, waving, and even sobbing. The mothers felt so elated; they applauded and nodded when Pastor Walker got to their pew.

Pastor Hall grabbed and hugged both Pastor Walker and Mother Walker. He then traded spots with Pastor Walker and Mother Walker, so that they would be facing the congregation. He took the microphone and faced both Pastor Walker and Mother Walker and said, "Today, Pastor Walker and Mother Walker, we the membership of One Way are begging your forgiveness for the pain, suffering, tears shed, self-doubt, anger, and sleepless nights we caused you."

Mother Walker raised her hand to the sky as Pastor Hall spoke, and she said, "God only knows."

Pastor Hall continued. "Pastor Walker, please step forward. We the membership of One Way are asking for your forgiveness; brother, we are truly sorry for the circumstances leading up to your departure from One Way. On this day, the church's 100th anniversary, we are begging for your forgiveness. Pastor Walker, will you accept our apology?"

The congregation eyed Pastor Walker as he took the microphone.

"Pastor Hall, I do accept your apology. As one man of God to another, thank you for having the courage to do this. This truly means a great deal to my momma and me. We still love One Way. Yes, Lord, I was hurt, but today I am healed. Today I am vindicated, exonerated, released, and delivered!"

Still standing, the members all applauded. The mothers, overjoyed, praised the Lord.

Pastor Walker went on. "One Way, you have done well. Pastor Hall called me last week and begged me to come. Naturally, I felt apprehensive. Pastor Hall put the needs of One Way before his own. I told him I did not want to intrude on his first day on the job, but he, being a fair and just man without an ego, told me there is no way he could be installed as your next pastor without making this right. On the day when he should shine, he opted to share his moment to shine with me. I cried that night just thinking about it. You know, he cares that much about little old me. He was thinking about and praying about somebody he didn't even know, for what would be one of the most important days of his life. God bless you, Pastor Hall."

With a nod Pastor Hall said, "Thank you."

Then, pointing at the mothers, a sobbing Pastor Walker cried out, "Mothers, I love all of you. I know you never stopped praying for me. I felt it. That day at the prison, I knew God brought you there, you hear me! God had to be working this out for all of our good."

The mothers smiled and nodded as they waved at both Pastor Walker and Pastor Hall. Pastor Walker, overcome with tears, gave the microphone back to Pastor Hall, who patted him on the back and gently said, "It's okay, Pastor; God knows your heart."

Pastor Hall moved on to Mother Walker and placed his hand on her shoulder, then tenderly asked, "Mother, will you find it in your heart to forgive One Way? We come to you today begging and pleading for your forgiveness."

Mother Walker took her glasses off and unbuttoned the top two buttons on her jacket as she grabbed the microphone from Pastor

Hall and said, "Yes, I will accept your apology, but, church, I need you to know the hurt and pain caused to my son. I will forgive, but I will never forget. Naturally, as a mother, when my child hurts, I hurt. As a mother I am a protector." Mother Walker moved to stand before the deacons and trustees, and she continued. "There were many times I wanted to come by this church and just slap a few people. Other times I rode by this church, and I wanted to set it on fire, burn it down to the ground!" Mother Walker shouted as she received frozen stares from the congregation. "Church, I was mad! I wanted to get even for what was done to my son." She moved toward the pew near the mothers. "Church, I then remembered this battle was not mine to fight; it was the Lord's. So I gave it to him. When I saw my son was at peace and had put this abominable period behind him, that was good enough for me. Let's be clear: it didn't happen overnight. But today, One Way and Pastor Hall, I will accept your apology. With that being said, Mother Mae, I owe you an apology. The day I saw you down at the Main Street Fish Market, I was a hurting and stubborn mother. From one mother to another mother, please forgive me. I was wrong and I am truly sorry."

Mother Mae nodded and smiled at Mother Walker.

Mother Walker returned the microphone to Pastor Hall and then gripped her son's hand. Pastor Hall passed the microphone to Pastor Walker and asked him to sing a verse of "Amazing Grace." Never had One Way filled its halls with more beautiful music to honor the Lord.

After Pastor Walker completed his verse, he and his mother took a seat up front. Pastor Hall then turned the service over to Sister Melody Note, the musicians, and the One Way Mass Choir.

Sister Melody shouted into her microphone as she tickled the ivories on the baby grand piano: "One Way! Put your hands together and let's have church. Let's start with 'Trouble Don't Last Always.' Get on your feet and help us sing it."

The congregation rose to their feet and sang praises to the Lord on this special day.

CPSIA information can be obtained
at www.ICGtesting.com
Printed in the USA
LVOW10s1549040118
561822LV00012B/1212/P